I0582015

HOT FOR

Her Bear

THE MONTANA GRIZZLIES 1

ARIEL MARIE

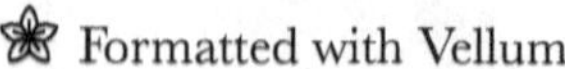 Formatted with Vellum

She was warned to leave the grumpy bear alone, but she couldn't help herself. Her curiosity was piqued. She wanted to see the bear roar!

Saffron Dakota knew she shouldn't have specific thoughts about her best friend's older sister. It was forbidden, but it didn't keep her from smiling at her.

Or making sure she was dressed up nice when around her.

Or randomly showing up to her cabin in the woods.

All of this, hoping the beautiful grizzly would show her just a wee bit of interest. Her friend would be pissed if she knew Saffron was crazy over her sister.

Dasha Prime couldn't believe the strong reaction her bear had to Saffron. After all of these years, it was clear what her bear was trying to tell her. It was something she had thought all along, but now her bear was roaring loud and clear.

Saffron was her mate, and Dasha would defend her woman against anyone who had a problem with it.

If you love steamy, wlw paranormal romance with a grumpy bear shifter and her sassy human mate, then you will enjoy Hot For Her Bear. This story was intended for mature readers only.

CHAPTER ONE

Saffron sat frozen in place and couldn't get a word in. Her date just droned on about himself and didn't even pause to ask about her. She was amazed he was able to even breathe. She tried to see when he inhaled but she couldn't tell.

"Our business is growing, and I've been able to sink a lot of my own money into stocks. That's how you truly get wealthy." Bishop Milligan was a bear shifter who really loved to hear himself talk. He picked up his hefty frosty mug and took a sip of his beer.

Saffron Dakota had only agreed to go out with

Bishop because she had just moved back home and thought it would be nice to catch up with someone she had gone to high school with.

She was so wrong. She would have been better off staying at home and counting all of the weeds growing in her yard.

"Do you even want to ask me about myself?" she joked. She stabbed her fork into her steak and brought it to her mouth. At least she'd got a good meal out of this. The steak practically melted on her tongue.

"What don't I know already? We graduated from school together, you went off to college at Stanford, got a job and lived in California for a while, and now you're back running your business." He sat proud of himself.

Well, damn. My life summarized in one sentence by Bishop Milligan.

"Yup, sounds like you know everything about me." Her voice dripped sarcasm, but he didn't pick up on it; his smirk blossomed into a full grin.

I need to do more with my life.

"What I meant was, do you want to know what I like, what I'm into?" She glanced at him and picked up her wine glass. She downed half of if in one swallow. Her gaze was already scanning the restaurant for the waitress for a refill. She was going to need more wine.

Lots of it.

"I can see you like wine." He snorted. "Why don't I take you to that one winery I hear everyone talking about."

Saffron's eyebrows shot up high. He thought they were going on another date? She knew better than to shoot him down now. He may up and leave her with the bill and stranded

Since he'd picked her up and driven.

She'd wait until he dropped her off before she broke the news to him. Grizzly bears were known for their tempers. Having grown up in Lurton, Montana, she was used to the bear shifter population. The town had a good mix of humans and shifters. Not just bears, it was full of wolf shifters, foxes, panthers, and a few tigers. She even knew a couple of the witches from the local coven.

Lurton was very diverse, and that was why she had moved home. Her family was still here, and it felt good to be back in the same place as her bestie, Pola. She hoped to find someone to settle down with and start a family. She hadn't had much luck in California. Besides, most city folk wouldn't want to live in a small town in the middle of Montana.

She had come home nine months ago to visit and had seen the local ice cream shop she and Pola had frequented as kids was up for sale. On a whim, she'd put in a bid on it—and won. She'd gone back to California, quit her job, sold her house, and returned to Lurton.

After a few months of hard work and renovations, the *Lick or Bite* was officially opened. She had purchased her cottage on the lake, and life couldn't be better. Now if only she could find someone to share her life with…

The bear shifter sitting across from her wouldn't be that person. If he was the only thing Lurton had to offer, she'd get a dog.

She caught the eye of the waitress and flagged her down. The woman came immediately without asking what was needed. She brought more wine and offered a sympathetic look. Lurton was small, and everyone pretty much knew everyone.

Saffron finished her meal, half listening to Bishop. She sat back and wiped her mouth on her napkin. The food might just be worth this torture.

"Want to sit at the bar for another drink?" Bishop asked.

"Not really. I'm tired." She faked a yawn. She

deserved an Oscar for best actress with this Academy Award-winning performance.

"Tired? From what? You own an ice cream shop." He barked a laugh and called for the check. "Are you tired from scooping ice cream for people and their kids?"

"Look, Bishop, I may not have a prospering business like yours, but it is something I'm proud of." She folded her arms in front of her and shot him a glare. That was it. She was so done with this date, she contemplated just getting up and leaving. She could call someone to take her home.

"Calm down. Can't you take a joke?" he scoffed.

He signed the receipt while the waitress glared at him, too. She'd witnessed his callous remark.

He handed the small slip of paper to the woman. "Some people are just so sensitive. Chill out."

He broke out in a fit of laughter again and slapped the table.

"What is so funny?" Saffron asked. She didn't even really know *why* she'd asked.

"Get it? Chill out? You own an ice cream shop." He grinned, but she didn't return his smile. He rolled his eyes and stood. "Fine. Let's go so I can take you home since you're tired."

"Thank you." She stood from the table and followed him out of the restaurant.

The drive to her cottage was spent with her quietly listening to him speak about his accomplishments with his business again. His father had started an outdoorsman company. It was very popular with them recently opening their fifth store.

His oversized pickup truck rocked as he turned down the gravel road. She had never been so excited to see her home come into view. There was something about having the lake facing her home and the dense forest at the back. If she didn't know any better, she would assume she was part bear shifter. She did love being outside and taking hikes on the trails.

Bishop parked next to her vehicle then faced her. She hoped he didn't think they were about to share a kiss.

"Thank you for dinner. It was nice catching up." She didn't wait for him and was out of the pickup. She slammed the door shut and went to race to her house, but somehow, Bishop had made his way to her side of the truck. She didn't know how a guy his size could move that fast or silent. Bishop had to be pushing seven feet tall. Most bear shifters were extremely tall and wide. There was not an ounce a fat on him. Apparently, he thought he was God's gift to women.

"Hey, I'm supposed to walk you to your door. I'm still a gentleman." He waved his hand for her to walk alongside him.

Saffron sighed and strolled along her stone walkway that led to her front porch.

"You never know what can be out here in the dark," he said.

She didn't say a word, not wanting to encourage more conversation. They arrived at her door. She took her keys from her purse and inserted one into her lock. She turned around and found Bishop standing directly behind her.

"Again, thank you for dinner. It was very good."

"Glad you enjoyed it. Maybe we can do it again. I had fun tonight." He smiled.

Saffron wasn't sure which parts were fun for him, but she was going to have to burst his bubble.

"Bishop, I don't think we should go out again." She wasn't going to be cruel, but this was where they would stop.

He sputtered, his eyes wide with shock.

"Have a good night." She spun around, slid in

the door, and shut it before he could get a word out. She locked up and breathed a sigh of relief. She kicked off her heels and padded into her living room. Like a coward, she left the lights off and peeked out from behind her front window's curtain and watched the big man stomp down the stairs and walk to his truck.

Once the lights from his pickup disappeared, she relaxed and headed to her room to change. After she was in something more comfortable, she'd call Pola and give her all the details of her date from hell.

"I could have told you it was going to be horrible, but I figured you needed to learn." Pola snickered.

"You are so mean." Saffron laughed. How could someone who was supposed to be a friend be so cruel? Best friends were supposed to have one's back. "But the food was good. We need to go there. Next time I look as if I'm about to make a bad decision, just hit me."

"I sure will. You didn't remember how much Bishop was into himself? His father spoiled the crap out of him, so he thinks everyone will want to worship the ground he walks on."

"I don't. I remember thinking he was handsome at one time, but now I'm good." Saffron stretched out on her couch and pulled her blanket over her over her legs. The television was on a random movie she'd found, but she had it on mute. It was past midnight, and the long day was officially catching up to her. "What do you have planned tomorrow?"

"Not much, we all are meeting at my parents' for a cookout. You should come."

"As in a party or just your immediate family?"

"Just my parents, brother, and sister."

"I don't want to intrude. That sounds intimate," she murmured.

Saffron thought of Pola's older sister, Dasha. The eldest Prime sibling was grumpy and always growled at her. Saffron had always assumed Dasha didn't care for her. She avoided Saffron and Pola when Saffron went to visit or spent the night. Dasha was ten years older than Pola, so it really could be that she didn't want to hang out with her younger sister and friend. That wasn't cool.

"Now you know my parents have always considered you their fourth cub when we were younger. If I tell Mom you didn't want to come, then you will hurt her feelings, and she might show up to your house and drag you over to theirs."

"You wouldn't dare." Saffron gasped. Mrs. Prime was crazy enough, she would come and bang on Saffron's door until she answered.

"Try me." Pola laughed.

"Okay. I'm coming."

CHAPTER TWO

"Dasha, be a dear and put this tablecloth on the patio table." Theola Prime shoved light-blue material into her arms.

"Why do we need this? It's just our family, or are we having company?" Dasha stared at her mother, who turned and went over to the stove.

Theola was a social butterfly and was always inviting people over to her house. Dasha had been under the impression that today was just a day for the Prime children to come spend an afternoon with their parents. It was a tradition their mother had started a few years ago. All of her children were out of her home and had become so busy she didn't get to see them as much as she would like to. So Theola began hosting dinner once a month. It was nice to see her siblings. It wasn't often she came down from her cabin in the mountains. She liked the quiet, serene nature and being away from people.

Shifters included.

Dasha was the eldest of the three cubs born to Amos and Theola Prime. She loved her family but she really didn't want to be bothered by her mother's friends. They were very nosy and always asking questions that were none of their business. Such as when was she going to settle down and get mated.

Well, that was a loaded question. She was a bear shifter, and she was waiting for fate to reveal that special person to her. She could be impatient and find someone to mate with out of convenience, but she did still believe in fate. Her parents were a fated pair. Watching them as she'd grown up, she knew she wanted what they had. She was willing to wait for it.

She just asked that fate hurried up. She was thirty-nine years old and wasn't getting any younger. Her birthday was later this year, and she would be forty. She would love to be able to run around with any cubs she and her mate would have. At this rate, her sister, Pola, or her brother, Junior, would be mated off and have cubs before her.

"You know how Mom gets," Pola said, entering the kitchen. Her sister breezed into the room with a wide grin on her lips and a twinkle in her eyes. She beelined it to Dasha and wrapped her up in a tight hug. "Hey, sis, I've missed you."

"You just saw me," Dasha grumbled. She bit back a smile and returned her younger sister's embrace. She knew she could be a grumpy bear, but it always felt good to know someone missed her.

"Excuse me. We haven't seen each other in two months." Pola gasped, pulling back. She moved over to their mother and kissed her on the cheek.

"That's not my fault. You didn't show up for dinner," Dasha scoffed.

"You should be seeing each other more than what you do," Theola said. "If something was to happen to me, who would feed your father?" She rested her hands on her waist. That same twinkle appeared in her eyes that Pola had.

Her family loved to joke. Dasha sometimes wished she was more like them. Instead, she was the oddball.

"Dasha would. You know I can barely make toast." Pola snorted.

"Where did I go wrong with you?" Theola sighed.

It was no secret that Dasha loved to cook. Living alone she had to, unless she wanted to starve. She loved to go fishing along the lake. There was nothing tastier than freshly caught fish cooked up the same day.

"You still didn't answer me on why we are dressing up the table," Dasha grumbled. She held up the tablecloth.

"Saffron is joining us today. She hasn't been by in a while, so I told her to come by," Pola said.

"I can't wait to see her. I heard her new shop is doing well," Theola grinned. She flew around the kitchen pulling items needed from the fridge.

"Oh." That was all Dasha could muster. She spun around and left the kitchen through the back patio doors.

Her mother had set up the table for them plus one. Dasha's hands grew moist at the thought of seeing Saffron. It had been a long time since she'd seen her sister's best friend. Her bear had sat up at the sound of Saffron's name. Her bear was in her lazy phase and resting while Dasha was in control.

Dasha moved some items off the oversized table and draped the cloth on it. She quickly placed the vase back in the middle. A slight wind blew, and she didn't feel like chasing the cloth to the middle of the yard.

Saffron was a beautiful brunette who was small and petite. At least by bear shifter standards. Dasha herself was six foot two, while her sister and mother were six foot even. Her brother and father topped out around six foot eight. Her sister's friend never appeared bothered by the height differences.

Dasha felt awkward around Saffron. She was always smiling, and when she was younger, she'd asked a ton of questions. Dasha wasn't a talker and preferred the quiet. Saffron and Pola were constantly at their parents' home, so Dasha would leave so she wouldn't have to be bothered by the younger girls.

But that wasn't entirely true.

Something had happened when Saffron turned eighteen. It was like a light was turned on. Dasha took notice of how pretty the young girl was. Dasha knew that wasn't right, she shouldn't be looking at her sister's friend like that. She was ten years the girls' senior, so she made sure she was never around, and if they had to be around each other, she never knew now to act, hence her gruff attitude toward her.

"Mom said for me to put this out here," Pola announced. She stepped outside with a glass pitcher of sweet tea and some glasses.

"Put it here," Dasha said. She tapped the middle of the table and turned away. She grabbed some other items that had been on it and put them back.

"You're not going to be mean to Saffron, are you?" Pola asked.

"What are you talking about? I'm never mean to her." Dasha put the plates her mother had left on the table around for each placing.

"You're always growling and glaring at her." Pola folded her arms. "Especially the summer after we graduated from high school. You always made her feel unwelcome."

"You two were teen brats, always home. What older sister wants to be bothered by her young sister and friend?" Dasha snickered. She shrugged and finished setting the table. "Plus, I'm a bear. I tend to growl at everything."

"You didn't even live here then!" Pola laughed.

"But every time I came over, both of you were

here." Dasha tried to smooth things over. She didn't want to admit to her sister that she had been attracted to her friend. Especially when they'd been out in the yard in their bikinis, sunbathing. She remembered ignoring both of them and just going into the house.

"Something is wrong with you." Pola shook her head, a small smile on her lips. She came over and hugged Dasha, then stepped back. "Okay, well today, be nice."

"I'll try." Dasha sighed.

Her sister's smile grew, and she spun around and raced back into the house. Dasha hadn't thought she had been as bad as Pola described, but her point had been received.

Leave me be.

Dasha took her time ensuring the table looked nice. She wasn't sure why, but she wasn't going to entertain the thought that it had something to do with Saffron joining them. Her bear paced, anxious to see Saffron. It had been a while since she had seen her.

Dasha went back into the house to see what else her mother needed help with, and she was put to work. Dasha got the grill started and soon had the meat going while her mother finished off the sides.

By this time, everyone was out on the patio, but Saffron had yet to arrive.

"Where's Saffron? I thought she was coming?" Amos asked. Her father sat back in his recliner on the patio, holding his cold longneck beer.

"Yeah, where is the little brat?" Junior asked. He sat next to their father while they were all catching up since the last time they had seen each other.

Dasha tried to not act as interested in the question. She faced the grill and checked on the large steaks her mother had purchased. Her mother had purchased enough food to feed a football team, but it was only to be the six of them. Bears had healthy appetites and could eat crazy amounts of food compared to humans.

"You know Saffron. That girl would be late to her own wedding." Pola laughed. She picked up her cell phone and typed off a message. "There, I just sent her a text asking where she is. She promised to come because I told her if she didn't, I'd tell Mom she refused."

Chuckles went around. Theola was very protective of her cubs. Even though Saffron wasn't her biological child, Theola would do anything for her.

"You children know me so well." Theola

stepped out onto the patio carrying another covered dish. She set it on the table and came to stand next to Dasha. "Everything okay over here?"

"Of course." Dasha snorted. There was no way she'd let meat burn on the grill under her watch. The aromas drifting up had her stomach and her bear growling.

"She's turning onto the street now, she said," Pola announced. She gave a squeal and jumped up from her seat. "I'll be back."

She raced off and disappeared around the house to go meet her friend.

"It's about time," Junior grumbled. "We won't have to wait to eat."

"I've taught you better manners than that." Theola laughed. She moved away from Dasha to gripe at Junior.

Dasha ignored their banter and tried not to think of her sister's friend.

She breathed a sigh of relief. She just hoped no one saw how she tensed up she was when Pola had announced Saffron's location. Her heart was pounding hard and racing. She picked up the tongs and took in the sight of her hands trembling. She gripped them tighter and checked on the ribs.

She had to act normal. She'd been around

Saffron before, but she didn't know why she was responding this way. Honestly, Dasha couldn't even remember the last time she'd seen Saffron.

Something was wrong with her. She held back a laugh and shook off this crazy feeling. Today would be a day to enjoy her family and relax. She had a ton of work to do when she returned home that would keep her busy for weeks until the next time she needed to come down from her cabin.

"Come on, boys. Get to the table. As soon as Saffron and Pola come back here, we can eat," Theola announced.

Dasha busied herself by taking the meat off the grill. Her stomach growled again, signaling how hungry she was. She had skipped eating earlier, knowing she was going to have a good meal waiting at her parents' home. She didn't want to do anything that would ruin her appetite. Now she was hungry enough to eat a horse.

Her father and brother had taken their seats at the table while her mother flew around removing the tops from the containers. Dasha went into the house to quickly wash her hands off. She had grease and black soot from the coals on her fingers. She stood in front of the sink with the cool water running on her palms, and her ears picked up her sister's voice.

"Look who I found?" Pola joked.

Dasha tensed. Her breath caught at the sound of a throaty laugh amongst the greetings from her family.

Saffron.

Dasha's breath escaped her. She took her time lathering up the soap on her hands. She focused on cleaning beneath her nails. She wasn't sure how she had so much stuff underneath them.

The door opened, and a new scent drifted across to her. Dasha snapped her attention to the door to see a gorgeous brunette standing there.

"Hey, Dasha," Saffron said, her gaze meeting Dasha's.

Every ounce of air in Dasha's lungs rushed out of her. She froze, taking in Saffron. The woman was dressed in a short cotton dress. It was white with black stripes, with only one shoulder and a belt that showed off her narrowed waist and wide hips. Her hair was pulled up in a messy knot on top of her head, and her toes were showcased by her black sandals.

Dasha's lungs screamed for her to breathe. She

blinked and inhaled and the scent that greeted her, sending her bear into a frenzy.

Mate.

Dasha took a step back, almost forgetting she was in the midst of washing her hands. Turning back to the sink, she flicked the water off.

"Hey." That was all Dasha would muster.

"I was just going put these in the fridge." Saffron held up two bottles of wine. Her killer-watt smile lit up her face. "I figured I should bring something. That's why I'm late. Cheap wine is better than no wine."

Saffron, unaware of the affect she had on Dasha, breezed past her and walked over to the fridge. She opened it and placed the two bottles in it before shutting it.

"Are you okay?" Saffron asked, a frown forming on her face. She reversed slowly toward the door, stopping inches from Dasha.

Dasha immediately kicked herself. She was doing it again—being awkward. She was still in shock by what her bear had growled. Could it be? Was Saffron her mate?

"Um, yeah. I'm fine." Dasha spun around and inwardly winced. Her voice had grown gruff. She snagged a drying towel to wipe her hands. She picked up on the sound of Saffron's footsteps heading toward the door. Once it shut, Dasha dared to glance in that direction. She tossed the towel down on the counter and leaned back against it, sinking her face into her hands.

Heavens above, was Saffron her mate?

Mate, her bear growled again.

This just couldn't be.

CHAPTER THREE

Saffron ambled alongside Pola, enjoying the fresh air and the nature. After dinner, they had decided to walk off some of their meal. The Primes owned a nice piece of land that had a path through the woods they owned. Mr. Prime had even outfitted it with little solar lights that lit up at night. The sun was almost down, and dusk was upon them. The sounds of the wild echoed around them.

"It was good seeing your parents, and your brother is still a goofball." Saffron chuckled.

Dinner had been interesting. Pola's parents had been the same welcoming bears as always. They never made her feel different being the only human. Lurton was a town where humans and shifters lived in harmony. That was one of the many reasons why she had decided to move home.

"That he is. I swear sometimes I think I was adopted." Pola chuckled.

"What?" Saffron laughed.

Her friend smiled and shook her head. "Just think about it. Junior is so outgoing, silly, and thrives on attention. My sister, on the other hand, is quiet, antisocial, and stubborn as hell." She sighed. "Then there's me."

"Oh, you are just perfect. If they had two of either of your siblings, I think your parents would have gone insane." Saffron wrapped an arm around her best friend's shoulders.

The Prime siblings couldn't be more different if they tried.

But there was something different about Dasha tonight. Normally, she just ignored Saffron whenever she was around. Saffron was used to her grunts and growls, but today, there wasn't as many as normal. She used to joke about there always being about five grunts and five growls on any given day when she was around Dasha. Today, Saffron had caught Dasha staring at her on more than one occasion, and there had only been one growl.

Weird.

"What's up with your sister?" Saffron asked quietly. She released Pola and continued walking alongside her. "I only got one growl from her today."

"Oh, I had a talk with her before you arrived." Pola grinned.

"What? Why would you do that?"

"Because I know she can make you uncomfortable at times. I know it's not her fault and she just doesn't like people, but she should be used to you by now."

"Well, I'm used to her growls and grunts after all these years. I need my ten," Saffron joked.

Pola fell into a fit of laughter.

"I thought maybe she was finally coming around to me or something." Saffron didn't know why, but her feelings were slightly hurt. She had thought Dasha was finally accepting her, but it was probably Pola threatening her. It had been a while since she had seen Dasha, and Saffron had to admit the woman was gorgeous. There was something about her dark hair and big amber eyes that drew Saffron to her. Then there was her height. Saffron had a thing for tall people. She didn't know why, but at five foot four, she always felt like a dwarf around the Prime family.

When she had walked past Dasha in the kitchen, she could have gone around the island in the middle of the room, but instead, she had chosen the path closest to Dasha. She had come within a hairsbreadth of touching her. She'd had to cock her head back just to look at the back of Dasha's head when she'd turned away from her.

Her core clenched at the thought of walking up behind her and wrapping her arms around the bear shifter's waist.

Saffron blinked.

Pull those thoughts in, girl.

Pola would probably burst an aneurysm if she knew the thoughts that were running through Saffron's head about her sister.

"Well, considering she did as I asked, we'll call it a win," Pola said.

"Maybe I should try to talk with her," Saffron murmured. She bit her lip, trying to think of what she could say to drum up a conversation with the grumpy bear.

"Just leave her alone." Pola waved a hand in the air. "My sister may be a lost cause."

They continued in a comfortable silence, but Saffron couldn't stop thinking about Dasha. She was determined to get to know the bear, and she needed to know why she kept staring at her. There was something in the bear's stare that took Saffron's breath away.

Saffron eyed her friend and decided she would keep her mouth shut. They arrived back at the house and found Junior and Mr. Prime sitting on the patio enjoying their beers. Mrs. Prime was relaxed on the chaise, working on one of her crossword puzzles she loved so much.

"Saffron, why don't you pour me a glass of that wine you bought," Theola said.

Pola walked over and took a seat and held up her hand. "I'll take one too." A wide grin spread across her face.

"Of course." Saffron stuck her tongue out at her friend and went inside.

The door shut behind her, and she froze in place. Dasha was at the sink washing dishes. The tall bear turned to her and leveled her with her amber eyes. They stared at each other without saying a word. Saffron unconsciously reached up and tucked her hair behind her ear. Dasha's intense gaze slid along her body. The heat from her gaze brushed Saffron's skin as soft as a lover's caress. She could almost feel Dasha touch her, but the woman had not taken her hands out of the water in the sink.

"What are you doing in here?" Dasha asked. She frowned and turned away from Saffron.

"I came to get us the wine. Do you want a glass?" Saffron asked. Her feet finally decided to move. She went over to the cabinet where the wine glasses were kept. The Primes' kitchen was still the same. She pulled out three glasses and paused, looking over her shoulder at Dasha. She was pleasantly surprised to find Dasha's attention on her ass. She bit back a smirk.

So the bear was checking her out. Dasha's eyes flicked upwards and met hers. Her face flushed as she realized she had been caught looking at Saffron's ass.

"Is it any good?' Dasha asked.

"Well, I've been told a time or two that it was very enjoyable and delectable." Saffron couldn't help but joke.

Dasha stared at her, a low growl emitting from her chest. Her eyes flashed feral for a moment before calming down to her normal amber color.

That was interesting.

"I meant the wine," Dasha grumbled.

Saffron grinned and grabbed a fourth glass and placed them on the island. She grabbed the wine out of the fridge and twisted the top. She didn't feel any shame about her cheap wine. It was good and always got her tipsy. The shifters wouldn't have to worry about that. Saffron had learned that little tidbit of information when she and Pola were in college. No matter how much they drank, Pola never got drunk. Apparently, her bear shifter metabolism burned through alcohol fast. Pola had to carry Saffron home several times.

"I know. I just had to tease you since you were checking me out." Saffron winked at her and poured hefty amounts in each glass.

"I was not," Dasha sputtered.

Saffron walked over and handed her a glass. Dasha's red cheeks and embarrassment were downright cute. Saffron was definitely attracted to the bear.

"Take a sip." Saffron jerked her head to the glass in Dasha's hand. She held her breath and watched Dasha sniff the glass first before taking a taste. She bit back a groan at the sight of Dasha's tongue sneaking out to slide across her bottom lip. "Well?"

Dasha raised the glass and looked at it, then switched her gaze back to Saffron. "It's good."

"I'm glad you like it." She smiled and turned to get the other glasses. She picked them up and headed back outside. She put a little more sway in her hips, sensing Dasha's gaze on her. She paused by the door and glanced over her shoulder again. Just as she suspected, Dasha's attention was glued to her bottom, a growl rumbling in her chest. The sound sent a wave of desire rippling through Saffron. Dasha's gaze slid along her frame until her eyes locked with Saffron's.

"There's another bottle in the fridge if you want more," Saffron said.

Dasha jerked her head in a nod.

Saffron's heart skipped a beat. She'd got Dasha to speak with her. This was a win. Saffron pushed open the door and went outside.

CHAPTER FOUR

Dasha stared at her canvas and didn't have it in her heart to work on it. She had always been artistic. She loved watching the brushes send colors along the blank canvas and create her masterpieces. Her nature paintings were always a big hit. She was on back order and needed to catch up. Her website was very popular, and she was lucky she was able to make a living doing something she loved.

Right now, this canvas wasn't going to finish itself. Blowing out a deep breath, she stepped away from her outdoor workstation. The few paintings she needed to get down was of the forest located behind her cabin. She was fortunate to have so much inspiration right in her backyard.

Dasha needed a small break. She walked over to the stairs and took a seat. She grabbed her water bottle and took a gulp. She had woken up at the break of dawn and finished another painting before she'd started the one she was stalled on.

There was a reason she wasn't feeling this picture.

A certain woman with big brown eyes, plump pink lips, and curvy hips was on her mind. It had been a week since the dinner at her parents' home. She just couldn't shake Saffron from her head. Dasha reached over and picked up the sketch book and pencil she had left on the top stair. She flipped open the book and took in the drawings of Saffron. She had thought drawing her sister's best friend would help purge her from her mind. Turning the pages, she reviewed her work. The first one was the exact image of Saffron when she had first entered the kitchen.

Dasha had captured her beauty perfectly. Her big round eyes, those plump lips, her face, and breasts. Dasha moved through the pages. By the time she got to the last one, she would admit it was from her fantasies. It was a drawing of Saffron naked, lying on a bed of grass out in the woods. A small smile played on Saffron's lips, and her arm was across her ample breasts, trying to hide them. Dasha had drawn her with lust heavy in her eyes.

It was as Dasha imagined her to look if she ever got the chance to have her mate.

Her bear was impatiently pacing in her chest. Her animal was confused why she hadn't taken her mate and claimed her last week.

Saffron was human, and she may have grown up with shifters, but she wouldn't truly understand what mating meant. Dasha had been craving the scent of her woman. She had been tortured the entire day, smelling it but unable to do anything about it, and when Saffron had caught her staring, she hadn't acted appalled. No, she had grinned and flirted with Dasha.

Turning the page in her book, she began drawing. This helped calm her bear any other time, but since the subject was her mate, her bear growled and pushed at Dasha's stomach—her animal was demanding to break out.

She allowed her imagination to run free. No one

would see the book, so she continued the picture she'd begun. Again, it was of Saffron naked. This time, she sketched her mate with her arms stretched above her. Those full breasts of hers were on display. Dasha concentrated on shading Saffron's areolas. She was so into her work that she almost missed the sound of a car pulling up to her house.

"Who is that?" she murmured.

She closed the book and set it down on the top stair. It was rare for someone to come visit her. Dasha loved her cabin because it was tucked away in the woods on the mountain. Only a few people knew how to find her. She walked around to the front yard and was shocked at who was stepping from the small sedan.

Saffron.

Dasha couldn't believe her mate was here. *Why* was she here? How did Saffron know where she lived? Dasha's gaze dropped down to Saffron's hands. She carried a cooler in one hand and a bag in the other.

"Hi, Dasha!" Saffron smiled and moved toward her.

She was in a summer dress with spaghetti straps over her shoulders. Her hair was pulled up in a high ponytail. It was an abnormally warm day out. Dasha's tongue was stuck to the roof of her mouth.

"I hope you don't mind me just stopping by."

"How do you know where I live?" Dasha was finally able to move her tongue.

Saffron stopped in front her. Dasha automatically inhaled, taking in the scent of her mate. Her bear, sensing their mate was near, gave a low, welcoming growl. Dasha inwardly cursed, watching Saffron's eyes grow wide at the sound. The slight hint of fear permeated the air. Saffron wouldn't understand her bear's growls.

"You don't need to be afraid."

"I'm not," Saffron replied. Her brown eyes grew darker. Her lips quivered slightly as she smiled at Dasha. "I'm quite used to you growling at me."

Dasha was captivated by her mate's beauty. Seeing her up close in the bright light of the sun, she saw details she had missed in her sketches. There were a few freckles underneath her left eye. There was a small mole on her top lip that begged for Dasha to kiss it. She ached to take her mate in her arms. She wanted to see if her lips were as soft as they looked.

"You didn't answer my question." Dasha

cleared her throat. Her hands balled into fists to keep from reaching for Saffron.

"Well, don't tell your sister I told you, but I came with her a couple of times when she needed to drop something off to you. I just never got out of the car," she said sheepishly. She moved closer and held her arms up. "This is for you. A gift."

Dasha stared at the bag and cooler. She panicked. Her mate had brought her gifts. Why would she do this? Did she know the fates had made them for each other? That when she put her claiming mark on her they would be connected together for all eternity?

"What is it?" Dasha didn't move. She was curious as to what her mate would bring her.

"Um, I caught a bunch of fish this morning and figured you would want some." She nodded to the cooler. "And as for this bag, I brought you some of the wine I took over to your parents' house. Pola told me you had drank the entire second bottle, so I thought you'd like some more."

Dasha wasn't sure why her sister felt the need to share what she had drunk. Saffron raised her arms again to offer up the gifts. Dasha took them from her.

"Thanks, but you didn't have to bring me gifts,"

Dasha grumbled. She didn't want Saffron to leave. Deep down, she was happy her mate sought her out. Dasha glanced back at Saffron and was taken back by her beauty. She thought quick and glanced down at her hands. "Do you want to stay? I can cook this fish up for us. That is, if you're hungry."

Saffron's face lit up, and she nodded quickly. This was new for Dasha, she never invited anyone into her home.

"I'd love to stay," Saffron said.

The wind blew and sent her dress flying up to expose her thighs. Dasha's breath caught in her throat at the sight of her creamy skin. Saffron wasn't the least bit embarrassed. She laughed and smoothed her dress down.

"Follow me. I was working in the back." Dasha spun on her heel and headed to the back yard. She paced faster at the sound of Saffron's footsteps on the grass. Dasha was very aware of the female behind her. The wind was carrying her scent to Dasha. It was an addictive aroma, and she wanted more of it. She wanted to nuzzle her face into the crook of Saffron's neck and breathe it all in.

"You have a beautiful cabin," Saffron said. "I would love to see the inside. Pola said you had recently done some renovations. I was thinking of having my kitchen and bedroom updated."

Was that the real reason she'd stopped by? To see the work that had been done on her cabin? It would make sense if she was wanting to see the quality of work of the construction crew. Dasha was slightly disappointed. But then she realized it would be her fault, she had never given Saffron a reason to seek her out before.

Hell, she had never really spoke to Saffron. This might be the most they'd ever spoken.

"So that's why you're here? You wanted to see what they did to my cabin?" Dasha asked.

They arrived at the backyard with Dasha guiding them to the porch.

"Sort of," Saffron replied.

They stopped at the bottom of the stairs. Saffron's cheeks flushed as Dasha watched.

She looked away from Dasha for a moment before turning back to face her. "To be honest, I came because I wanted to see you."

Dasha's eyebrows jerked up high. She hadn't expected that to come out of Saffron's mouth.

"Oh." Dasha didn't know what to say. So she did what she always did when Saffron was around

—ran. "I'll be back. I'm going to take these inside. Make yourself comfortable."

Dasha didn't wait and went inside her cabin. She blew out a deep breath and headed straight to the kitchen. She set the cooler and bag down on the island. She peeked inside the cooler to look at the fish. She had an outdoor kitchen out on her back porch. They could cook and relax outside since it was nice out. She knew Saffron liked the outdoors. That would be perfect.

Their first date.

Her bear was slightly satisfied with this. She just wanted to jump ahead and claim Saffron.

She's human, and we can scare her, she snapped to her beast. That was the last thing they needed. If Saffron had really come here to see her, then Dasha would take full advantage of her being there.

She dashed around her kitchen looking for her wine glasses. She found two and then gathered what she would need to prep and cook the fish outside.

What else could I make with it?

She tossed the wine in the fridge so it could chill for a little. An idea was coming to her on what side dishes she could make.

A calmness took over.

Her mate had come to her. Saffron had to have

felt something for her to want to come see her. She was going to take advantage of Saffron being at her cabin. It was just the two of them, and Dasha would make this special.

She snagged a basket her mother had given her and put all her seasonings, knives, oils, and other items in it. Lifting it, she decided she would need to make several trips. Satisfied with her plan, she headed back outside.

CHAPTER FIVE

"So far, so good," Saffron murmured. She had been so sure Dasha would have sent her away. She couldn't believe Dasha had accepted that she had come just for her. She hadn't lied about wanting to get some work done on her house, but she figured she would need a strong reason to be there.

With Dasha in the house, it gave her a little time to explore the yard. Dasha had a couple of easels set up.

Saffron had always known Dasha was a talented artist, but these paintings were amazing and so life-like. The details were superb. Saffron stepped closer to the one that was finished and then glanced at the real deal behind Dasha's home, and it was an exact replica.

The other painting she had barely started with a few bold strokes painted.

Maybe she would ask Dasha to capture her property and the lake. She would love to own a piece of Dasha's work. The lake would look beautiful on canvas with the sun shining high. Saffron turned and walked over to the porch and decided to sit on the stairs.

She could hear Dasha slamming the cabinets in her kitchen. Saffron's presence rattled the bear shifter. What she was really expecting, she wasn't sure, but Dasha had piqued her curiosity. She wanted to get to know her. There was something about her amber eyes that drew her to the bear.

Dasha was hot.

There, she'd admitted it. There was no use for her lying to herself. She had always thought so, and if she got a chance with Dasha, she would take it. Saffron took a seat on the stairs, feeling that distinctive tug of arousal.

What would Dasha's lips taste like?

Did she like kissing? Saffron hoped so. She loved it and wouldn't mind offering her lips up to Dasha.

Her breasts tingled as she imagined Dasha's lips surrounding her nipples.

Saffron shook her head and rubbed her arms that were suddenly covered with goosebumps. She needed to get herself together before Dasha came back outside. She moved up higher on the stairs so she could rest her feet on the bottom step. Her hand brushed something, so she turned and saw a sketch book sitting on the landing.

"What's this?" she murmured. Saffron was nosy by nature and wanted to see what Dasha was working on. Her eyes widened when she opened the book to the first page.

It was a drawing of her.

Her mouth dropped open, but no sounds came out. She flipped to the next page and found another drawing of herself. As she continued on, the drawings became more risqué. The final ones were of her naked and in sexy poses.

If she'd ever questioned whether or not Dasha had ever thought of her, she had her answer.

From the looks of the pictures, Dasha had really been thinking of her. She paused and glanced over her shoulder at the door. Dasha was still fiddling around in the kitchen.

Well, if Dasha had drawn these pictures from

her head, then Saffron wanted to give her real-life inspiration. She set the book down and stood from the stairs. She disrobed until she was completely naked. She sat on the plush grass and waited for Dasha to come outside.

She bit her lip, waiting for the bear shifter.

It didn't take long for Dasha to come out the door. The bear had a pile of items in her hands. She froze, her gaze landing on Saffron.

Her gaze caressed Saffron's body, leaving her feeling a hot rush of desire flooding her.

"Saffron…" Dasha's voice ended on a hitch. Her gaze came back up and met Saffron's. "What are you doing?"

"Well, I was sitting here admiring your work." She jerked her chin to the book on the steps.

Dasha's eyes followed and paused on the sketches. It must have fallen open when Saffron had tossed it down. The slight breeze turned the pages, leaving it open to the drawings of a very naked Saffron.

"I figured since you were using me as a subject, I would give you the real thing. Not that those aren't good, but there's nothing like seeing the real thing up close and personal."

Dasha still remained frozen in place. Her amber

eyes were wide, her nose flared. She inhaled, and Saffron knew the shifter would be able to scent her arousal. Just the thought of Dasha thinking of her and sketching her from memory had her turned on. What had gone on in her head when she had drawn her naked?

"You went through my book." Dasha's voice was husky. She moved over to the counter and set her items down before walking to the top of the stairs. She appeared recovered from her initial shock. She bent down and picked up her book. "I can explain."

"There wouldn't be any need. A picture, they say, is worth a thousand words." Saffron's lips curled up in the corner. She shook a playful finger at Dasha. "All this time I thought you hated me."

"I've never said I hated you," Dasha replied. She walked down the stairs and sat on the bottom one near Saffron's feet.

"Could have fooled me," Saffron muttered. She grinned and leaned back on her elbows. She dropped her legs open, revealing her most private parts for Dasha. "Like I said, if you want the real thing, I'm right here."

Dasha didn't take her eyes off Saffron's center. She opened her book to a blank page. She snagged the pencil that was resting near where the book had been originally. She drew big strokes, and Saffron wished she could see the picture come to life. The heat in Dasha's eyes was rising. Her gaze was like a warm caress to Saffron's skin. She could feel everywhere the shifter's attention lingered.

Saffron's body temperature skyrocketed. She bit her lip, staring at the bear shifter who was focused on sketching her. Saffron's body trembled, her arousal growing. She could feel the slickness grow in between her legs. Her core pulsed with need.

Saffron dug her fingers into the soft grass. Dasha paused, her nose flaring as she inhaled. A low grow vibrated from her chest. She had sensed Saffron was aroused, and the fact that she knew turned Saffron on even more. Her hips thrust forward, seeking what she needed. She eyed Dasha, wishing she'd come and bury her face between her legs.

What would it feel like to have her tongue sliding between her folds? To have her tug on her clit?

Saffron's head dropped back, and she imagined it. A whimper escaped her. Her ears picked up on the sound of Dasha moving. She lifted her head and found Dasha had set the book down and was crawling toward her on her knees.

"Your scent," Dasha murmured. Her focus was locked on Saffron's center. She moved to kneel between Saffron's legs.

"What about it?" Saffron asked. She was curious as to how her scent could affect Dasha. From the looks of it, she was under a spell. Her hands rested on Saffron's thighs.

"It's calling me," Dasha admitted.

Her hands, callused, slid along the soft suppleness of Saffron's thighs. The feel of her roughness elicited a shiver to ripple through Saffron. She dropped her thighs completely open for Dasha.

"I need to taste it." Dasha's voice grew huskier. The amber flames in her eyes revealed her bear was near the surface.

Saffron practically screamed for her to go ahead, but she kept herself as calm as she could, considering her heart was racing.

"Go ahead. Taste me," she whispered.

Saffron watched with bated breath. Dasha lowered herself to lie on her stomach, putting her at eye level with Saffron's pussy. Saffron's eyes fluttered closed once Dasha's mouth covered her pussy. She moaned, arching her hips. Dasha's tongue parted her slit. She gasped at the sensation of her tongue sliding through her soaked center.

Another growl ripped from Dasha. Her hands tightened on Saffron's thighs, holding them open. She feasted on Saffron as if this was her last meal. Her hot mouth closed around Saffron's clit.

Saffron's arms gave out, unable to hold her up any longer. She lay back on the ground, basking in the sensation of Dasha's mouth tasting her most intimate parts. Her breaths grew faster, making it harder for her to breathe. Her legs were pushed up and out of the way by Dasha who grew more frantic. Her tongue dipped into her warm channel before skating down to her dark hole. She whimpered, enjoying every bit of this moment.

A cry escaped her when Dasha sank a finger into her. The bear shifter's mouth was back on her clit, suckling it into her mouth. Her finger pumped in and out of Saffron's channel before she introduced another one. She pushed them deep inside Saffron while increasing the pressure of her suckling. Saffron's body writhed, unable to lie still. She thrust her hips forward, meeting the motions of Dasha's hand. Her cries escaped her, growing louder. She had never been one to be quiet during sex, and with the way Dasha was consuming her, she had to let the world know how good the woman was eating her pussy.

Tremors racked her body. Her hand dove down, and she entwined her fingers in Dasha's thick hair. Her hips gyrated against Dasha's face. Her eyes shut tight while her she felt herself balance on the edge of ecstasy. She cried out, Dasha's fingers pounding inside her. Another finger pushed forward, stretching her out. She gasped, loving how full she felt.

A sharp pinch on her clit sent her skyrocketing to the heavens. She screamed out, her orgasm taking over her. The intense electrical current rippled its way through her body. She gripped Dasha's hair, grinding herself onto Dasha's face.

Warm tears slipped from her eyelids. She fell back, panting. Her body jerked from the lingering aftershocks of her climax. Her body was flushed, her nipples beaded into tight buds. Everything on her was extremely sensitive. She opened her eyes and gazed down, meeting Dasha's intense stare. Her bear shifter rose and crawled over her, bracing herself over Saffron. The look in her eyes was something Saffron had never seen before.

Dasha leaned down and pressed her lips to Saffron's. Her tongue forced its way into Saffron's mouth. She gently stroked Saffron's tongue with hers. Saffron reached up and wrapped her arms around Dasha's neck, pulling her down on top of her. She returned Dasha's kiss with the fever that Dasha gave. She wrapped her legs around Dasha, trapping her.

Dasha broke the kiss and stared down at Saffron. Her hand came up, and she trailed her fingers down Saffron's cheeks.

"Mine," she growled. Her eyes burned even brighter. She pressed a hard kiss to Saffron's lips then left a trail of hot kisses along her jawline and down to her neck. She nuzzled her face into the crook of Saffron's neck.

Saffron arched up toward Dasha and turned her head automatically. She wasn't sure why, but she needed to let Dasha have access to the column of her neck and shoulder. Dasha's warm tongue skated along her skin, sending shivers through her.

"God, you have too many clothes on," Saffron muttered.

She released her legs to allow Dasha room to move. Her finger went to the edge of the bear's shirt, and she tugged on it. Dasha helped her, drawing it over her head, then tossing it. The rest of her clothes flew off before she came back to

Saffron. They groaned simultaneously when their naked bodies slid along each other. Dasha's body covered hers, their breasts pressing to each other.

Their mouths fused together in a deep, passionate kiss. Their legs became tangled until Dasha spread Saffron's far apart. She straddled Saffron, holding her gaze. Saffron's breath caught at the feeling of Dasha's wet pussy lowering onto hers. Dasha reached between them, parting Saffron's labia to expose her clit. She rocked her hips, bringing hers to rest on Saffron.

"This is mine," Dasha said.

The possessive nature sent a ripple of desire through Saffron. She held Dasha's gaze and gave a nod. If sex between them would always be like this, Dasha could have her.

Saffron thrust forward, wanting to feel their cores slide against each other. They both were extremely wet, allowing them to glide together in harmony.

Dasha increased her pace, her hand cupping Saffron's breasts. She broke their stare and focused on Saffron's mounds. Her hands covered them, massaging them. Saffron rested her hands on Dasha's waist. She had already had one hard climax and could feel another one coming toward her. She was unsure how, but all she knew was that Dasha knew how to draw pleasure from her.

"So perfect," Dasha muttered.

She pinched and pulled on Saffron's nipples. She dropped her head back down to Saffron and captured her lips. Her body covered Saffron's as they writhed together, their bodies moving in sync with each other. Saffron skimmed her hands over Dasha's back, and they came to rest at the nape of her neck. Dasha dominated the kiss, just as she did their lovemaking. Saffron turned all of her pleasure and her body over to her.

Saffron would have never guessed her trip would leave her naked, being fucked by the woman she couldn't get off her mind. She would admit she'd been infatuated with Dasha for years, and to find out the woman had been thinking of her, too, left her feeling elated.

Dasha pushed Saffron's head to the side, presenting her neck again. She licked the column, her tongue coasting along her shoulder. Saffron had the sudden need for Dasha to bite her.

She had been around bears enough to know what a bite would mean.

Was she Dasha's mate?

Was that why she kept saying "mate?"

Dasha lightly nibbled her before sucking onto her skin. Saffron gasped, her hips thrusting harder against Dasha's. She reached down and held on to Dasha's bottom, bringing her to her. She was almost at the point of no return again. Never had she had two orgasms so close together. She dug her nails into Dasha's round ass, needing her to be closer.

"Dasha," she moaned. Saffron was desperate for that euphoric feeling of her release. She needed it.

"Saffron," Dasha groaned.

The sound was music to Saffron's ears. She loved to hear Dasha taking her pleasure.

"Yes," Saffron hissed.

Dasha nipped her harder, not enough to break the skin, but enough to send an electric current to Saffron's pussy. She arched her neck, offering it. Their movement became jerky as they both pressed harder against each other.

"I want you to come for me."

It was as if that was all Dasha had to say. Together, they fell into the abyss of pleasure, reaching their orgasms together. Saffron's muscles tightened while another scream erupted from her lips. Dasha buried her face into the crook of her neck, her cry muffled.

They lay together, unmoving, while coming down from their journey. Saffron panted, trying to catch her breath. She held on to Dasha, not wanting her to move. She loved the feeling of the larger woman lying on top of her. Their centers were still resting on one another. It was the best feeling she ever had. She smiled, not wanting to leave. They would certainly need to have a talk.

Dasha was going to have to explain this "mine" business.

But for now, Saffron was content in her post-sexual bliss underneath the woman who had made her body sing.

CHAPTER SIX

Dasha was unsure what to think. She had given in to her animalistic nature and took the woman who was her other half. It had taken everything she had to keep from sinking her fangs into Saffron's shoulder and claiming her.

Dasha lifted her head and gazed down upon Saffron. She caught sight of the dark mark forming on Saffron's fair skin. A deep, satisfying growl erupted from her. It wasn't her claiming bite, but it was her mark. She liked seeing Saffron marred by her. It did something to her—and her bear who was very possessive.

Saffron blinked, her eyes meeting Dasha's.

Dasha reached out and brushed her hair from her face. Saffron's beauty had always left her speechless.

How is she mine?

"Well, here I was hoping for a meal and received so much more." Saffron smiled. She reached up and cupped Dasha's face and brought it down. She pressed a chaste kiss to Dasha's lips.

Dasha's bear growled again.

She wanted more.

"Is that so?" Dasha asked. She kissed Saffron again. It had been something she'd wanted to do for so long, and now she had full access to her. She could still taste Saffron's cunt. Her taste was something that Dasha would crave. It was sweet with a hint of tang, and she wanted to go back down and get another taste.

"You do know I've been crushing on you for years but never had the balls to approach you," Saffron admitted.

Her smile disappeared as she stared at Dasha. The truth was evident in her eyes. Dasha could sense if she were to lie, but at the moment, her mate was speaking the truth.

"I just licked your cunt and I didn't see any balls there."

Saffron stared at her for a moment before bursting out into laughter. She shook her head and pulled Dasha down for another kiss.

"You always amaze me," she said, her lips brushing against Dasha's.

"I'm amazed by you," Dasha said.

The fates above had gifted this beautiful woman to her, and somehow, she was going to have to tell her. Maybe she would do it after they'd eaten. That exact moment, Saffron's stomach made itself known.

"You came here looking for a meal. Let me feed you." Dasha untangled herself from Saffron and stood.

She reached out a hand and assisted Saffron up. She brought her woman to her, holding on to her. Dasha's bear was extremely possessive and didn't want Saffron to be even a few feet from her. She pushed her bear back down who was trying to break free.

"I've certainly worked up an appetite." Saffron's lips curled up into a smile.

Dasha realized she always wanted to see her mate happy and smiling. Her mate deserved the world, and Dasha was going to make sure she damn well got it.

That was, if she accepted the mating bond.

"Well, come so I can fry the fish."

"It's getting late. We can do that tomorrow." Saffron pressed close to Dasha.

She was already planning for their next meal together, and that pleased Dasha and her bear. But her mate was right, it would take some time to gut and clean the fish before she would be ready to cook it. She glanced up at the sky and took in the rolling clouds that were coming in. A storm was not too far away.

"Fine. Come, let me cook you something else that will be quick."

They gathered their clothing, the easels, the paintings, and her notebook, and went inside. Dasha dashed back out onto the porch and collected the supplies she had taken outside and took them back inside. She dropped them off on the counter and found Saffron about to put her clothing back on.

"Leave it off."

Dasha stalked around the island to where her mate stood. She reached out and took the dress from her hands.

"I want you naked," Dasha murmured. After she'd fed her mate, she had plans for the two of them. She was a shifter, and being naked was normal for them. Over the years, she had lost plenty of clothes from her bear shifting before she could take them off. Shifters weren't bothered by nakedness. It was as common as breathing in air.

"Oh?" Saffron's eyes widened.

"Yes," Dasha said.

She may have been shy and unsure if her mate wanted her, but after their lovemaking outside, she'd had a taste of her mate, and she was going to demand more. Her mate's body was to be her playground, and she would ensure she was well pleased. That was what drove shifters.

Mate, provide and please.

All of which she was ready to do.

The only problem would be telling her sister that she had not only fucked her best friend, but she was also fated mates with her.

"Okay." A silly grin appeared on Saffron's lips. She allowed Dasha to take the dress from her. Her body was perfect and should never be covered up. She pressed against Dasha, wrapping an arm around her. "Whatever you have in mind, I'm down for."

"Good." Dasha dropped her head and took Saffron's lips in another kiss. It deepened, and she pressed Saffron to the counter.

Feed mate, her bear growled.

Right. She was about to do something. The mating bond was already pulling her to her mate. She eased back and rested her forehead on Saffron's. "Food. I need to give you food."

"I had already forgot about that." Saffron blew out a deep breath. A small smile played on her lips. Her hand came to rest on Dasha's sternum. "It doesn't have to be anything fancy."

"Well, let's see what I have that will be quick and easy." Dasha took Saffron by the hand and led her to the fridge.

They went through it and decided on cold-cut sandwiches and chips. Dasha enjoyed them standing side by side constructing their sandwiches. Working alongside her mate in a comfortable silence seemed natural. As if they had been doing it for years.

"Do you have any Cokes?" Saffron asked.

Dasha nodded and grabbed two cold cans from the fridge and glasses.

Saffron shook her head. "I don't need glasses. Can is perfectly fine."

Dasha grinned. She, too, preferred to drink straight from the can.

They took their meal and sat on the stools at the island. Dasha couldn't stop stealing glances at Saffron as they ate.

"Is everything to your liking?" Dasha asked. Her bear worried about their mate and if she was pleased with the food. If not, she would cook something for her.

"Everything is fine. Matter of fact, it's perfect." Saffron smiled. She reached out a hand and rested it on Dasha's knee.

Dasha's gaze dropped down to her small, soft hand. She had already come to the conclusion that she loved having her mate's hands on her. Seeing Saffron freely touch her opened the pit of desire that was close to boiling over. "Who would have thought me and you would end up here?"

Saffron slowly caressed Dasha's thigh while popping a chip into her mouth, Her warm brown eyes studied Dasha.

"I've always thought you were beautiful," Dasha admitted. After all these years it felt good to get this off her chest. She turned to Saffron and took her hand in hers. She wasn't good with words. She was always one who best expressed her feelings though her artwork. It was why her works were so popular. People could connect with her paintings. Now she wanted to say something clever and romantic, and her tongue stuck to the roof of her mouth. She frowned, unable to think of anything, so she just blurted out the first thing that came to her mind. "You don't care that I'm so much older than you?"

"Not at all. I think that makes you sexier." Saffron didn't hesitate with her response.

She gave Dasha's hand a squeeze before guiding it between her legs. She spread her thighs wide enough to allow Dasha's hand to cup her silky-smooth mound. Dasha immediately slipped a finger between Saffron's slit and found her drenched, she inhaled sharply. Had she been paying attention she would have smelled her mate's arousal.

"And I have a thing about older women who are bear shifters."

"What about my sister?" Dasha asked. She had to address the elephant in the room. Her hand remained where it was, her half-eaten food forgotten.

"Well, that depends. Was this just a one-time thing?" Saffron leveled Dasha with a serious gaze.

"No," Dasha exclaimed. There was no way she was giving up her mate. She would find the perfect way to tell Saffron. She didn't want to just blurt it out, she needed it to be special. What was between them would be forever. Dasha wanted to ensure that Saffron would accept her. She and her bear would have to prove they were worthy of Saffron's love.

Her animal sat up, ready for the challenge.

She was very competitive and determined. Her bear wasn't worried. Dasha wished her human side was as confident as her animal.

"Then we will have to tell Pola. She would be upset if we didn't." Saffron made it sound so simple. But Dasha had to admit her sister was the levelheaded one of the Prime siblings.

"I agree. I wouldn't want to deceive my sister."

"But if we want to take a couple of days to explore what is between us, I don't think it would hurt." Saffron's eyes twinkled with mischief.

This was the Saffron Dasha had always been intrigued by.

She rocked her hips against Dasha's hand. "And I want to know how long you've thought I was beautiful?"

Now it was Dasha's turn to blush. She shouldn't admit it, but she refused to fib to her mate. Starting off lying wouldn't be healthy. She slipped her finger farther into Saffron's slit, gathering her honey before trailing it up to her swollen nub. Saffron's eyes widened as she held Dasha's stare. A low moan slipped from her lips. Dasha was in awe with how Saffron's body responded to her. It had to be the mating bond. Her human mate wouldn't understand how intense the bond was until she received her claiming mark. The bite would trigger a response in her that would reveal to her the deep connection she had with Dasha. Shifters sensed it before the mating, and it always drove their animals crazy. Dasha was getting the sense and would have to claim Saffron soon. Otherwise her bear would only focus on claiming their mate until she had succeeded.

"The first time was the weekend you came to the lake with our family when we went boating," Dasha said softly. Her finger strummed Saffron's sensitive pink button. Her mate's eyes darkened, becoming filled with lust. "We were out on the lake on my dad's new boat, and you were wearing a new bikini you had just got."

"That was years ago," Saffron breathed. She settled against the backrest, opening her legs wider for Dasha. A beautiful blush spread down her neck and over her full breasts. Her brown nipples were puckered into buds. Her chest rose and fell with her small pants. "I remember that weekend, I was sixteen."

"I know." Dasha closed her eyes, ashamed. She shouldn't have been eyeing Saffron at that age. It was then she'd decided to stay away from the young girl, she was ten years older and had no business having carnal thoughts crossing her mind. "And it wasn't right, so I pushed you away. I thought if I was mean, you wouldn't come around me and would leave me alone."

But that hadn't been the case. Saffron and Pola were the best of friends and did everything together. Most times it seemed as if Saffron spent more time at the Prime house than her own. Once Dasha had moved out on her own, she didn't have to worry about her sister's friend.

"All the things I imagined doing to you would have landed me in jail." Dasha's lips curled at the expression on her mate's face. Her parted lips, her wide eyes were so sexy and had her bear pacing.

"Well, what's stopping you now?" Saffron exhaled slowly. She snagged her bottom lip with her teeth. A whimper escaped her.

Dasha stood from her chair and moved closer to Saffron. She rested her free hand on Saffron's shoulder while sinking her fingers into her warm, wet channel. Her muscles contracted around Dasha's finger. She withdrew it and pushed two inside Saffron's delicious-smelling cunt. She held Saffron's gaze while she fucked her with them.

"You're staying the night then." It wasn't a question but a command. Her bear was growing aggressive, and Dasha decided to go with the flow.

"You couldn't kick me out if you tried." Saffron moaned.

Her eyes fluttered shut before quickly reopening. Her hips moved in tandem with Dasha's hand. She leaned over and captured Dasha's nipple with her mouth. Her tongue teased Dasha, leaving her groaning, and she increased the pace of her hand. Dasha's free hand slipped to the back of Saffron's head, holding her in place. Saffron's juices flowed over her hand.

"Yes," Dasha hissed.

She twisted her fingers around, looking for that certain point that would send Saffron skyrocketing to the heavens. Saffron released Dasha's breast with a loud popping noise cutting through the air. Her mouth widened, and her head fell back. Her eyes were begging for her release. Dasha wanted to give her mate what she was seeking. She brought her thumb up to press it on Saffron's clit.

Dasha gripped Saffron's hair and tilted her head back to allow her to swoop down and capture her lips with hers. Saffron's body stiffened, her orgasm overtaking her. She swallowed Saffron's scream. Saffron's hands clamped down on Dasha's arm. She broke the kiss, panting, trying to breathe. Her hips jerked, still riding Dasha's hand.

Saffron opened her eyes once she'd come down from her euphoric journey. Her lips tipped up into a satisfied smile. Dasha's animal growled at the look of pleasure on her face. This was something she would need daily. She withdrew her fingers from Saffron, bringing them to her mouth. The taste of her mate exploded on her tongue. A fierce growl ripped from her. She pulled Saffron from the chair and held her close.

"We are not done yet." She towed Saffron behind her and headed to the bedroom.

CHAPTER SEVEN

It had been two weeks since Saffron had bravely showed up at Dasha's home unannounced. They had been inseparable since. They were learning all about each other, and Saffron was happier than she had ever been.

Soon they would need to tell Pola about them. She hated keeping secrets from her best friend. They spoke practically every day, and it was killing her to not tell her about the budding relationship with Dasha. Would Pola accept them being a couple? Saffron didn't know, but they would find out soon.

"How many scoops?" Saffron asked. It was late in the afternoon, and the shop would be closing soon. On Sundays, she closed the shop early to allow her employees to be able to enjoy some part of their weekend. One more hour, and she'd be locking the doors.

The little girl with twin pigtails turned to glance at her father. She had to be around five years old and was a cutie pie. Her father chuckled and shook his head.

"She can only handle one scoop." He grinned.

His daughter's shoulders slumped, leaving Saffron to feel bad for the munchkin.

"How about if I make it a big scoop?" Saffron winked at her.

That earned her a shy smile and a nod.

All kids wanted big ice cream cones when they came to her shop. The Lick or Bite was known for high-quality ice cream. Saffron ensured she served the best.

She scooped out the chocolate ice cream the little girl had asked for and piled it high on the waffle cone. Her eyes were wide as she took it from Saffron.

"Melody, what do you say to the nice lady?"

The little girl's father rested a hand on her tiny shoulder.

She glanced up at him, having already stolen a few licks of the chocolate ice cream. He nodded toward Saffron. She turned and smiled.

"Thank you." Melody's voice was soft, but Saffron heard her.

"You're welcome, darling." Saffron was a sucker for little kids. She hoped to have a few in the future. She wasn't getting any younger and wanted to experience motherhood. She switched her attention back to the little girl's father. "What will you be having?"

"Oh, nothing for me. This was all about Melody." He smiled and pulled out his wallet.

They walked over to the register where she rung him up. The duo soon left the shop, leaving Saffron alone. She would take advantage of the slow, steady trickle of customers to clean and begin the breakdown process. She took some of the less popular flavors and storied them properly in her large freezer in the back.

As she worked, she couldn't help but to wonder if Dasha was going to stop by and see her at the shop. All day she couldn't stop thinking about her beautiful bear shifter. If she didn't know any better, she would think she was catching feelings for Dasha. Saffron had enjoyed all the time they'd spent together.

Another family soon made their way into the store. Her heart leaped when she caught sight of Dasha entering behind them.

"Welcome to Lick or Bite. What can I get you?" Saffron greeted them with a smile.

Dasha took a seat at one of the vacant tables. She was patiently waiting for Saffron to finish with her customers. Once they were rung up, they left immediately. It was a beautiful day outside, and Saffron was sure everyone wanted to take advantage of it.

She wiped her hands on her waist apron and came from around the counter. Dasha hadn't said a word since arriving. She'd quietly watched Saffron as she'd worked.

"Hey." Saffron smiled, making her way to Dasha.

The bear's intense gaze didn't waiver from her. Saffron's heart rate increased, and she could feel the signs of her body growing aroused. Whenever she was around Dasha, she was in a constant state of arousal. Something about Dasha triggered this reaction in her. She didn't know what it was, but she liked it.

"Can I get you anything?" Saffron asked.

Dasha's eyes glowed even brighter. Saffron was getting good at recognizing Dasha's expressions. This one in particular was very familiar. It was the look she gave before she ravished Saffron's body.

"Just you," Dasha murmured.

She pushed back slightly from the table as Saffron came to stand by her. Dasha patted her thigh softly, giving Saffron the command to sit on her lap. Saffron didn't hesitate and was immediately engulfed in Dasha's warm embrace. Dasha gently tugged on Saffron's chin to bring her face close.

The kiss they shared was soft and gentle. It always amazed her how Dasha could be gruff and ornery one moment, then the next minute sensual and caring. The gentleness of the kiss blew her mind. It almost brought tears to Saffron's eyes. She could feel the emotions and feelings Dasha had for her. They broke away and stared into each other's eyes. Saffron didn't have to reach up and feel her mouth. She sensed her lips were swollen from the passionate kiss.

"Wow." That was all Saffron's mind could

process. Dasha was constantly shocking her with something spontaneous. "What was that for?"

Dasha shrugged. She reached up and trailed a finger along her bottom lip. Her attention was locked on Saffron's mouth.

"I just wanted to show you how much I care for you."

Saffron's heart skipped a beat. For Dasha to be the type of person who had a hard time expressing her feelings verbally, the kiss said it all.

"I care for you, too," Saffron admitted. Things between them were progressing fast, but she didn't care. Everything felt right between them. She pressed a kiss to Dasha's lips. "How was your day?"

The shop was emptied out, and there wasn't much left for her to do. Dasha's work was so interesting. The fact that she was able to sell her artistic creations and make a living off it was mind-blowing.

"Actually great. I have a series of paintings I did a while ago sell for five times the asking price. There was a sort of bidding war going on." Dasha smiled. She perked up, excitement lining her face.

"Wow, that's amazing. How was there a bidding war?"

"A few galleries around the world apparently had their eyes on my work. I had a hard time deciding if I was going to sell them, but then I decided if I did, I wanted it to go somewhere where they could be on display and not just in a private collector's home."

"I have to see them," Saffron gushed. She brushed Dasha's thick locks away from her face. "Especially before they go."

"Sure. I have them in my storage." Dasha's shyness revealed itself. Her blush deepened as it always did when she spoke about herself or her work.

"Why don't you come over tonight and we can celebrate." Saffron stood and turned to her. She motioned to the empty shop. "I'm supposed to close in twenty minutes. I can just go ahead and close up now, then we can head to my place. I have a nice bottle of wine, some steaks…"

"Sounds good to me. Need any help here?"

"Nope. It won't take me long." Saffron smiled. She quickly made her way behind the counter so she could finish. There were a few more ice creams that needed storing, and she just needed to close out the register.

Maybe today they could define what they had between them. They hadn't really talked about their status, and Saffron knew something special was between them. Dasha was the only one who brought out certain reactions and feelings in her.

Could it be that they were fated mates?

She'd been around shifters enough to know about fate and the mating business. She actually respected it. Humans weren't so lucky. It could take a person five tries before they found "the one" and even then could still get it wrong.

Fate took care of everything.

The sound of the door opening had her turning to it. Her smile faded when she saw who entered.

Bishop.

"Looks like I made it in time." He confidently strolled into her shop with a cocky grin on his lips.

"I'm sorry, Bishop. I'm closing a few minutes early." She glanced over at Dasha who was staring at the large bear with a narrowed gaze.

"That's okay. I wasn't here for the ice cream anyway." He stopped at the counter, resting his hands on it. She was sure he thought he appeared sexy, but for her, he fell short.

"Then why are you here?" she asked, playing

dumb. She had hoped he had forgotten about her and his request for a second date. Apparently, he didn't believe she would turn him down.

"I told you I wanted to take you out again."

"And I told you I didn't think we should go out again."

"Do women really know what they want?" he scoffed.

Dasha's low growl echoed though the air.

Bishop stiffened and glanced over his shoulder at her. "Dasha, didn't see you sitting there."

"She said she didn't want to go out with you." Dasha's voice was low and to the point. Her amber eyes were glowing.

Saffron recognized it as a sign that her animal was close to the surface.

"What are you? Her bodyguard?" He snickered.

"That's none of your business." Dasha stood and came to stand next to him.

Saffron panicked slightly. She didn't want Dasha trying to go against Bishop. He was much bigger than her in their human form, and she was certain his bear was larger, too.

He glanced between her and Dasha. His eyes widened suddenly as if a light bulb had gone off.

"Wait? You're sniffing around Saffron?" He barked a harsh laugh and slapped a hand on his thigh. "Don't you think you're a little too old for Saffron? And what can you offer her? Certainly not cubs."

Dasha's face turned beet red. Her growl was loud and fierce.

Saffron raced around the counter and made a space between the two growling bears. Bishop's fangs were on full display.

"Bishop, please leave. Who I see is none of your business." Saffron rested a hand on both of their chests, trying to separate the two. She gave him a firm push back. She couldn't afford to have them shift and tear up her store. She had sunk all of her money into this dream of hers.

His hard gaze met hers.

"What you need is a real man," he snapped. He backed away from her and strode to the door. He paused with one hand on it and turned back to her. "Once your little guard bear isn't around, we can have a decent conversation."

"There won't be a need for a conversation, Bishop. There is never going to be an 'us.'" She stood her ground with her hands on her waist. She felt a figure behind her.

Dasha.

Saffron met Bishop's hard gaze before he stepped out of her shop. She rushed over to the door and locked it. She didn't want to chance him turning around and coming back.

"I'm so sorry," she breathed. Saffron leaned back against the door.

Dasha had a murderous look on her face. If she had the chance, she would probably go after Bishop.

"He doesn't get a pass on being an ass," Dasha ground out. She ran a hand along her face. Her bright-amber eyes were glowing. Her chest rose and fell fast.

Saffron walked over to her and rested her hands on her forearms. "Don't worry about him. He has being an ass down to a science."

"Someone needs to teach him a lesson," Dasha grumbled.

Saffron chuckled and rubbed Dasha's forearms. She could see the bear in Dasha calming down.

"It won't be us. Come. I'm almost done, and I promised you a celebration at my house." Saffron wanted to distract Dasha from Bishop. She rose and pressed a kiss to Dasha's lips.

Her bear turned her attention to her. Her eyes softened, and her shoulders relaxed.

"Give me two minutes and we can leave."

She backed away from Dasha, gave her wink, and rushed behind the counter. Today was a special day, and she wasn't going to let Bishop ruin it. Today was a day for them.

CHAPTER EIGHT

Dasha breathed in her mate's scent. She nuzzled her neck and wrapped her arms around Saffron's waist. She couldn't get enough of her. Back at the ice cream shop, she had been ready to defend her mate against Bishop. Someone needed to put that asshat in his place. He was a menace to the bear community. Just because he had money didn't mean he could treat people anyway he wanted, or be rude.

"How can I cook if you have me wrapped up in your arms?" Saffron glanced over her shoulder. She stood in front of the grill cooking their steaks.

Dasha chuckled and tightened her grip slightly before releasing her. Saffron had changed clothes when they had arrived at her home. She was dressed in a light-pink tank top and a pair of gray cotton shorts. The outfit was driving Dasha crazy. Both would be easy to remove.

"I guess I can let you go for now." She pressed a kiss to Saffron's bare shoulder and moved away to take a seat on one of the lounge chairs on her back porch. Dasha looked forward to her time with Saffron. Her bear was growing more possessive of her and wanted to be around her all the time. Having Bishop make moves on her woman didn't sit well with her. She wanted to put her mark on Saffron so all bears and any other shifter would know that her woman was taken.

"This will be a simple meal," Saffron announced. She walked over to the table and took out the bottle of wine she had sitting on ice.

"Those are always the best," Dasha replied. She didn't care if their meal was cereal, she just wanted to be near Saffron. She was quite sure she could survive on what was between her mate's legs anyway. She licked her lips, the memory of Saffron's honey coming to mind.

"Get your mind out of the gutter, ma'am." Saffron swatted her shoulder. She grinned and poured Dasha a glass.

"I didn't even say anything!" Dasha scoffed.

"I can't read your thoughts, but your facial expressions are very open," Saffron murmured. She poured herself some wine and took a sip. "For instance, when I know you are thinking of sexy time, your eyes glow bright. Matter of fact, any time you are passionate about something it happens."

Dasha sat back, never having realized she was so easily readable. Or maybe it was just that her mate was very in tune with her. Again, fate was a show-off. This little bit of information Saffron had shared just proved how compatible they were with each other.

"I've learned certain things about you, too." Dasha gripped the back of Saffron's thigh and brought her close to her. Again, she found herself needing to touch Saffron. She skated her fingers along the back of her naked leg. Thanks to the tiny shorts Saffron had changed into when they'd got to her home, Dasha had a hard time concentrating with Saffron's soft supple legs on display.

"Oh yeah? Like what?" Saffron groaned. She

reached over and tucked thick strands of Dasha's hair behind her ear.

"For one, I know you love when I nibble on your inner thigh. The noise that comes from between your lips let me know that." Dasha's fangs threatened to descend. She slid her hand up to stop at the meat of Saffron's ass. Her shorts revealed her ample cheeks, and Dasha wanted to rip them off. Saffron's breaths were increasing as she listened to Dasha.

"What else?" Saffron whispered.

"When you get nervous, you bite your bottom lip. That just drives me crazy."

"Why?"

"Because I want to nibble on your lips." Dasha paused and sniffed the air. Something smelled as if it was burning.

Saffron stiffened and glanced over her shoulder.

"Shit!" She darted back over to the grill. She set her glass down and opened the lid with smoke escaping to the sky. A sigh escaped her. "Thank goodness. We're good. Nothing is burned. I must not have cleaned the grill off good."

Saffron finished cooking, and it didn't get past Dasha that she was keeping her distance. Dasha was pleased to see that she affected her mate as much as she did. Saffron had their food plated and on the table. It was as she had promised. A simple dinner of steak, baked potatoes, salad, and wine. It was a perfect meal to celebrate.

Everything was just perfect.

The series she had sold was one she had painted a few years ago. She had promised Saffron she could see it before it was packaged and shipped off. Dasha was a little nervous. The series was personal, and she had never known how much until now. Dasha had named it A Midnight's Dream.

There were three paintings of the same scene with a bear standing on the edge of the lake staring at a reflection in the water. In the water wasn't the sight of the bear but of a woman. In the first image, the woman's face was blurry with ripples of water distorting her face. The second picture, the woman's face was more defined, the ripples not as strong.

The third picture revealed the face of the woman to be Saffron.

Fate was telling Dasha something.

At the time she'd created the paintings, she at first hadn't recognized the woman to be Saffron, but as time had gone on and she'd continued to perfect them, she'd realized who the female was. She had been confused but just thought that it was a coincidence, but now she understood what her subconscious was telling her.

Saffron was her mate.

They ate in a comfortable silence. Dasha loved the quiet of the atmosphere. She loved Saffron's property. She had the best of both worlds surrounding her home. The woods and the lake.

"You did a good job. My steak is cooked just how I like it." Dasha motioned to her plate. She preferred her steak to be medium to rare.

"Thanks." Saffron's face lit up with excitement. "I was nervous cooking for you."

"Why?" Dasha's eyebrows rose high. Her mate shouldn't be nervous in front of her. She wanted Saffron to always be comfortable around her.

"You're such a good cook, and I'm just okay." Saffron's cheeks flushed a warm rosy color.

She smiled, and Dasha knew without a doubt that she loved Saffron. She had gone through a lot to ensure this dinner was perfect for them.

"It's not the food that matters, it's the company that makes the celebration." Dasha reached over and took Saffron's hand in hers. She entwined their fingers together and gave a tight squeeze. "And you're all that I want."

Saffron's eyes widened.

"What are you saying?" Saffron whispered.

Dasha's bear paced inside her chest. This was the moment she had been waiting for. Her bear wasn't going to let her wait anymore.

"I think you know what I'm saying." Dasha smiled gently at Saffron and continued holding her hand. She didn't want to risk the chance that Saffron would try to run away. "You are my mate, Saffron. You belong to me and I to you."

Tears appeared in Saffron's eyes. Dasha froze, fear filling her heart. Had she read Saffron wrong? Was this just a fling to her? She hoped not. Her bear would go crazy if Saffron turned them down. They would have to let her go. They couldn't force a mating. No matter what, she would always love Saffron and would want to see her happy, even if it wasn't with her.

Saffron wiped her cheeks, clearing the trail of tears. Dasha grew anxious waiting for Saffron to say something.

"Did I just say something to make you sad?" Dasha couldn't wait any longer. She wiped her hands on her legs and immediately missed the warmth of Saffron's hand

"No, you didn't. These aren't tears of sadness. They are tears of joy." Saffron chuckled.

Dasha relaxed slightly, but she still didn't understand why her declaration would trigger a tearful response.

"I'm so glad to hear that your bear identified me as your mate." Saffron pushed back and came over to Dasha.

Her smile widened as she straddled Dasha. Saffron wrapped her arms around Dasha's neck and promptly fused her mouth to Dasha's. Her bear roared, loving that their mate was accepting of their claim. Dasha immediately took control of the kiss.

Her animal demanded she claim her mate now.

Possess her.

Put her mark on her so the world would know Saffron was her woman. She immediately deepened the kiss. Her tongue swept into Saffron's mouth, stroking her tongue. Dasha reached up and held Saffron's head in a place while she thoroughly kissed her. Saffron leaned into the kiss, returning it with a hot fever of her own. Her moans filled the air.

Dasha pulled away and trailed hot kisses along

Saffron's neck. She nipped the spot she was dying to sink her fangs into to put her mark.

"This is where I'll put my mark," Dasha growled. Her gums burned and stretched as her fangs pushed through.

"Do it," Saffron whispered.

She cupped Dasha's face and stared into her eyes. Dasha's chest rumbled from her bear's agreement with Saffron. Her mate's lips were swollen, and the scent of her arousal was thick in the air, distracting Dasha. She moved her gaze from her tasty lips and met her eyes.

"There is nothing I want more than for you to claim me," Saffron said. "I can feel it here that I belong to you." She pounded on her chest above her heart.

A snarl escaped Dasha, her gaze dropping back down to Saffron's shoulder. She skated her hands down Saffron's body and rested them on her waist. She could do it now. One bite, and she would bind her woman to her forever. She pulled Saffron as close to her as possible, leaving no room between them. Saffron's hot core rested on her stomach. The scent of her arousal grew stronger, and it was consuming Dasha.

She reached up and brushed Saffron's hair away

from her shoulder. Saffron pulled her shoulder strap to the side, revealing her smooth skin. She tilted her head, giving Dasha full access to her. She watched Dasha, her eyes filled with trust.

The sound of a car door slamming shut broke Dasha from her haze. Saffron stiffened.

"Who the hell could that be?" Saffron murmured.

Dasha's bear growled. She wasn't sure why, but her animal sensed something. Dasha always trusted her animal.

If it was her sister, then they would tell her now and come clean about their relationship.

"Let me go see who it is," Saffron whispered.

"We go together," Dasha replied.

The hair on the back of her neck stood to attention. Dasha didn't have a good feeling about this. Her bear was going into protective mode, ready to defend her mate. Saffron stood from Dasha's lap and brushed her hands on her shorts. Her nipples were pushing through the thin material of her shirt.

Dasha's bear issued a warning growl. Her animal wasn't too pleased at being interrupted from claiming their mate. Dasha stood and took Saffron's hand in hers. She didn't care who had arrived at the home. She was ready to tell the world. As soon as this person was gone, she'd take Saffron inside and claim her properly. Once her fangs sank into Saffron's flesh, they would make love all night to consummate their new mating. The bond between them would be sealed and the carnal urges would take over.

"Whoever it is, they cannot stay long," Dasha growled.

"I agree." Saffron muttered. She leaned against Dasha.

They walked around the house and headed to the front. At the edge of the house, Dasha pulled to a stop. A growl rippled from her chest at the sight of Bishop standing by his pickup truck.

"What is he doing here?" Saffron groaned.

"Don't worry. He's leaving."

"Get rid of her," Bishop snapped. His gaze landed on Dasha, a scowl forming.

The audacity of the man to think he could come and demand Saffron to do anything. Dasha's hand clenched into a tight fist.

"Go home, Bishop. There is no us!" Saffron shouted.

Dasha was impressed that her mate was brave enough to stand up to Bishop. But unfortunately, there was only one way to get a point across to him.

Violence.

And her bear was only too happy to provide what he needed.

"You expect me to believe that you would pick this old bear over me?" he scoffed. His smile didn't reach his eyes. He had to be deranged.

Saffron had shared with her how they had only gone out on one date. Why would he be so insistent that Saffron be with him when fate had shown her that Saffron belonged to her?

"I don't care what you believe. Get the fuck out of here." Dasha's voice ended on a growl. Her patience was wearing thin. She sensed her animal rising to the surface and she was ready to turn herself over to her beast. It was obvious her bear was going to have to do the talking. Her beast wasn't the slightest bit scared of Bishop's bear. He may outweigh her, but she was ready to face the bear head-on in a challenge.

"No one was talking to you, Dasha. This is between Saffron and me," he sneered. He pushed off the truck and took a few steps toward them. "Give me another date, Saffron. You'll see I can give you more than she ever could."

"Bishop, there is no second chance. I made that clear before and I guess I have to be very blunt,"

Saffron exclaimed. She held up a hand, warning him to stay away. "I don't want you."

His eyes darkened, and a growl rippled through the air. Dasha raced forward and snagged Saffron by the arm. She met him with her own growl, pushing Saffron away from them.

The bears were coming out to fight.

CHAPTER NINE

Saffron stumbled back from the force of Dasha's shove. Dark-brown fur sprouted out onto Dasha's arm. Her growls grew louder as she allowed the change to overcome her. Saffron grew worried as she watched the two of them shift into their bear forms. They fell down onto their hands and knees. Their clothing fell away in shreds, drifting off to the ground. Snarls and groans filled the air until they'd both completed the change.

Bishop's bear stood on his hind legs, towering over Dasha's smaller bear. He let out a roar that left Saffron taking a few steps back. Her heart raced, making it hard for her to breathe. She had never been this close to a pissed-off bear before.

Dasha didn't back down. She stood on her hind legs, a foot shorter than Bishop. Her bear roared back, apparently unfazed by the size difference. She couldn't let Dasha fight Bishop. He would tear her apart.

A scream erupted from Saffron. Bishop swiped his massive paw at Dasha who dove and avoided it. He fell onto all fours with his fangs exposed. He tried to sink his teeth into Dasha, but she retaliated by landing a blow with her paw. Her claws dug into his face, leaving a trail of blood coursing down his fur.

Saffron couldn't bear to watch this.

She spun around and took off running around her home to the back to grab her cell phone off the table. She had to get help for Dasha. A roar shook the ground. Her heart all but leaped into her chest.

Who was that? She couldn't tell if it was Dasha or Bishop.

She skidded to a halt at the table and snagged her phone. Her hands shook so badly she almost dropped the device on the floor. Saffron inhaled and tried to calm down her racing heart.

She dialed the local emergency number and jogged back to the front.

"Nine-one-one. What's your emergency?" a nasal voice answered.

"Yes, my mate is getting attacked by another bear," Saffron cried out. She arrived at her front yard and didn't see any signs of Dasha and Bishop. Their snarling was now coming from the woods next to her property.

"Your mate is a bear also?" the voice asked calmly.

Saffron wasn't sure how he could remain cool at a time like this when it came to bear-on-bear violence.

"Yes, she is. Her name is Dasha Prime. The bear attacking her is Bishop Milligan."

"What? I'm sending someone now. Where are you located?"

She gave him her address and walked toward the woods. She just hoped Bishop wouldn't harm Dasha.

If Dasha was injured or killed, she would never forgive herself. She picked up speed at the noises from the fight. It didn't sound too good. Roars, growls, and snarls were all she heard.

"Ma'am, we have an enforcer unit located not

too far from you. They should be there in a few minutes."

"She may not have a few minutes. They've disappeared into the words." Saffron stood at the edge of the trees. A loud crash echoed as if a tree fell. She took off running without a care for her own safety. She had to help Dasha.

"Ma'am, I'm going to have to suggest that you go and wait in your house. The enforcers will handle the situation."

"That may be too late," she snapped. Saffron followed the sound of the fight. She almost toppled over a fallen tree. The roots were torn and exposed. It hadn't stood a chance against two brown grizzlies fighting. They were massive beasts with jaw-dropping strength. "Someone has to help her."

Saffron disconnected the phone and sped up. The fighting wasn't too far from her. She feared what she was going to see. Bishop was much larger than Dasha, and he could really do some damage. She came to the clearing, and a cry escaped her lips. The two bears were on their hind legs, battling each other with their sharp claws. They were ferocious, their fangs and mouths bloodied. They were close to a cliff that led to a steep drop into the river that fed into the lake in front of her home.

Saffron's heart seemed to leap into her throat. She dare not cry out for she knew it could distract Dasha and she didn't want to give Bishop any more of an advantage than he already had. Saffron looked around to see what she could use as a weapon. She couldn't stand by and watch her mate lose.

Her gaze dropped to a pile of rocks on the ground.

Look at fate.

Saffron had a mean arm back in the day. She'd played a little soft ball when she was younger. Without thinking twice, she made her way to that pile. There were all different sizes and looked as if they would do damage.

At least to humans. She didn't know if it would even hurt an eight-foot-tall grizzly bear.

She wondered if she still could throw and hit a target.

"We're about to find out," she muttered. Tossing her phone to the ground, she picked up a rock and tested out its weight. The stone was smooth and the size of a tennis ball. Saffron aimed and cocked back her arm, sending the rock flying toward Bishop. It hit him square in the shoulder. "Yes!"

Her celebration was quickly cut short when he turned his fierce eyes to her. He growled, baring his fangs as if to warn her off. Dasha took advantage and swiped at him with her claws, catching him off guard. He spun back to her with a roar. They swiped at each other, and now his back was to the cliff

"I'm not afraid of you. Leave my mate alone!" Saffron shouted. She bent down and grabbed two rocks, one in each hand. They were smaller but would do. She was determined to help Dasha. Her mate would not fight Bishop alone. They would defeat him together.

Saffron got closer and angled herself to where she wouldn't hit Dasha. She got to the right spot and sent the first rock sailing. It hit Bishop in the face. It stunned him, and he stumbled back a few feet. Saffron took another step and threw the other. She was excited that she appeared to still have her aim. This one hit him square in the chest. His attention was fully on her. He roared and fell down on all four legs.

"Oh, shit!" Saffron backed up, looking around for somewhere she could run and hide. Of course, she wouldn't be able to outrun a pissed-off grizzly bear. Saffron's heart raced, but she held his gaze. A low roar shook the ground and almost sent Saffron tumbling.

Dasha.

She rushed toward Bishop and slammed into his side with all of her might. They fell onto the ground, a mix of fur and fangs. They rolled around, viciously snapping and clawing one another.

Saffron searched for something else she could use but came up empty-handed.

Where the fuck are the enforcers?

According to the dispatcher, they weren't that far away. She didn't know how much time passed, but it seemed as if it had been forever. Her attention landed back on Dasha and Bishop, and she froze. Dasha had backed Bishop all the way to the edge of the cliff. Her mate now had the upper hand. She rose on her hind legs and towered over the other bear who was on all four legs. She swiped her deadly claws at him, catching him on the face. He shouted and slashed out at Dasha but missed.

The smaller bear continued her assault, forcing him to the edge. He sprang forward unexpectedly and sank his fangs into Dasha's shoulder. He jerked them backward, the move sending them spiraling over the ledge. Bishop's eyes connected with hers before they disappeared from sight.

"Dasha!" Saffron screamed.

She sprinted toward the edge with her heart all but in her throat. She fell to her knees and crawled to the edge and peeked down at the river below. She breathed an air of relief at the sight of Dasha's smaller bear lying along a little landing on the cliff. There was no sign of Bishop. He must have fallen into the water.

Saffron turned her attention back to Dasha. She was all that mattered. Saffron couldn't care less *what* happened to Bishop. He should have left her alone.

"Dasha!" she called out.

The bear didn't move. She was lying at an odd angle on her side. Worry filled Saffron as she waited for Dasha to show some form of life.

"Hello there" a voice shouted from the trees behind her.

Saffron whirled around and took in two men and a huge bear ambling towards her.

"It's about time. Dasha's down there." Her voice ended on a hiccup. She turned back to look at her bear and found her in the exact same spot. Saffron bit her lip and tried to see if Dasha's chest was rising and falling. She was a little ways down the side of the cliff, and Saffron couldn't tell.

They came to stand next to Saffron and peered

over the ledge. Saffron eyed the bear who stood in the middle of the men. He glanced at her and offered a snort and a head jerk. Her eyes widened at his greeting.

"I don't see any signs of Bishop," the guy closest to Saffron murmured.

"That's one hell of a fall." The other one shook his head and motioned to the bear. "Sega, you think you can get down to her?'

The bear growled and looked around before jogging over to an area he could go down. Saffron wasn't sure he would manage since he was so big, but he didn't seem to be worried about it.

"Are you sure one of you shouldn't be going down since you're in your human form?" she asked.

The one nearest to her chuckled.

"Sega is the most sure-footed of us all in his bear form." He held out his hand to her, a grin spreading across his face. "I'm Nick, an enforcer for the clan. This is Abe, and that's Sega who is almost to your mate."

She took his hand in a firm shake, then turned her attention back to Dasha. He was right, Sega was taking the side of the cliff as if he were a goat. He confidently made his way to Dasha. They waited patiently for him to arrive at her side.

Saffron exhaled once he paused near Dasha. He nudged her with his snout.

Dasha jacked away, lifting her head off the ground. Saffron smiled, her vision growing blurry. She blinked back the tears watching the bears below. She didn't know what was being said between them with the low, nonthreatening growls leaving them, but she was just happy Dasha appeared okay.

Dasha sat up and shook her head. She looked around at where she was before she raised her head. Their eyes connected, and relief was apparent in her facial expression. This woman had almost fallen to her death, and Saffron had been worried about her.

Saffron's heart swelled with love for the bear shifter.

She wiped the tears from her face when she accepted the reality that she had fallen in love with Dasha just that quick.

She'd always believed in things happening for a reason. Deep inside, she knew that what this was between her and Dasha was meant to be.

As long as Dasha was well, she would make sure her bear claimed her.

Tonight.

CHAPTER TEN

Dasha took a deep breath and regretted it. Her lungs burned, and she was quite certain she had broken a few ribs. Sega, the enforcer, stood protectively over her. She pushed up on all fours. Her animal was careful to watch her step. She wasn't sure how she didn't fall straight into the water along with Bishop.

The last thing Dasha remembered before she'd blacked out was his sharp fangs sinking into her shoulder and tugging her forward. She hadn't been able to pull away from him due to his hold, until they were tumbling down the cliffside. She had let loose a roar that was swept away by the wind as they'd fallen. She'd landed hard and blacked out.

Sega watched her as she stood. She wasn't sure how he had made his way to her. The incline was steep and rocky. He must be a super bear.

Shift.

The command came through in her head. She met Sega's eyes and nodded. He would know the best way to get her out of here. With him being a member of the enforcer team for their clan, she trusted him. She'd known him pretty much all of their lives. She inhaled sharply and begged her animal to release the control over their body.

No.

Her bear was stubborn. She was injured and cranky. The process of healing had already started. The wound to her shoulder was no longer oozing blood. The other claw markings from the fight were healing also. It would take a day or so before she would be completely healed.

Give me control, she snapped. She closed her eyes and pushed her bear back. Even though her animal could come to the forefront, Dasha was still the stronger of the two. She transformed back to her human body. Her bones reshaped, popping into place as they shortened. Her fur receded into her skin. Within a minute, she was resting on her hands and knees feeling like a newborn baby.

Her breaths came in pants. She rested for a moment before lifting her head to meet Sega's patient eyes. There was a single question in them.

"I think I should be able to make it," she whispered. The fight had taken a lot out of her.

He moved forward so she could place a hand on his shoulder. She inhaled sharply and regretted it. The burn rippled through her lungs. She winced and held on to his shoulder. She looked back up to see Saffron standing with Nick and Abe.

Dasha was glad Saffron had been safe. She was going to have to talk to her mate about trying to interfere in a bear fight.

She distracted Bishop, her bear growled.

Dasha ignored her animal. Saffron should have just stayed completely out of the way and hid. There had been a reason she had drawn him away from Saffron's house. She hadn't wanted to chance them doing any damage to her property.

But the moment he had moved toward Saffron, Dasha had lost it. Her bear went feral at the thought of him getting closer to her mate. She would die before she would allow any harm to come to Saffron.

Dasha gripped Sega's thick fur and followed him along the path he had taken to get to her. She stumbled a few times, but she was able to right her footing. She was naked but didn't care. She was a bear shifter, and nudity was second nature for her.

Dasha held on to Sega while he continued to lead the way up toward the others. They grew closer to the top, and she straightened her back to try to appear strong for her mate. She wanted Saffron to see her as a capable mate, someone who would be able to protect her.

The moment they reached the top, Saffron was at her side. Concern was evident on her face. Dasha held her arms open, and she flew into them. Dasha held back a grimace from the pain. She couldn't care less about it and would rather have her mate in her arms.

"You're hurt," Saffron exclaimed. She leaned back and glanced up at Dasha's face.

"I'm fine," Dasha breathed.

"You are not." Her gaze landed on Dasha's shoulder.

The skin had been torn from Bishop's bite. It wasn't as mangled as before with her healing process kicking in. Her body was riddled with wounds and bruises. All of them were no longer bleeding. She ached but was sure another shift and rest would help her heal.

"We're going down to the river to see if we can find any trace of Bishop," Abe said. He came to stand by Dasha. He was a friend of her brother's and had been an enforcer for a few years now. "I'm glad to see you're okay, Dasha. Bishop is a tough son of a bitch. We're going to find him."

"You think he would have survived the fall?" Saffron asked in disbelief.

"I'm pretty sure. We bears are hard to kill. The fall may have injured him, but since we don't see a body, we're going to assume he landed in the water."

"Don't worry, ladies. We'll find him," Nick said.

Sega gave a growl as if to echo his agreement. Dasha gave them a nod to save some of her strength and not speak.

"If we need you, we know how to find you." Abe gave her a salute before turning away. He stood with Nick, conversing in a low, hushed manner.

Dasha trusted the enforcers would find him.

The alpha of their clan wouldn't take too kindly to Bishop attacking her and still going after her mate. It didn't matter if Saffron carried her mark or not, she belonged to Dasha. He'd overstepped a line that he would have to answer to the alpha about. Dasha would log the complaint and share her encounter tonight with their alpha.

Edwina Fang, better known as Eddie, was a fair alpha who upheld the laws of their clan. She was tough and would ensure justice was served for Bishop breaking the laws. The Fangs and the Primes were two families who were close and the first to settle in their small town of Lurton, Montana. Eddie would hear her out and be on her side.

Bishop would pay for what he'd done.

"Will you be able to walk?" Saffron asked. She wrapped her arm around Dasha's waist and held on to her.

"If it kills me," Dasha muttered.

"Nobody's dying," Saffron snapped. Her eyes were wide and red as if she had been crying.

Dasha groaned, loving the feel of her mate's hands on her naked flesh. Now wasn't the time to be thinking of the thought coming into her head. She was injured, but it didn't keep her from wanting her mate.

Her fangs pushed at her gums, straining to descend once again. The scent of her mate, the feel of her, and the sound of her voice had her wanting to claim her at the moment.

Not right now.

At least they could go back to Saffron's home now.

Dasha brought Saffron closer to her and dropped a kiss on her forehead.

"I promise I'm fine," she said.

Saffron jerked her head in a nod.

"Let's get back to your place. It may take me a little bit, but we'll do it."

"There's no rush," Saffron said.

"There really is. We were interrupted in something we have to finish." Dasha's voice went low. She rested her hand on Saffron's shoulder and brought her lips to Saffron's ear. "I need you, Saffron."

Dasha felt the tremor ripple through her mate. She smiled, pleased by her human's reaction. Dasha scented the slight arousal of Saffron's cunt drifting up to her. She licked her lips, anticipating the taste on her tongue.

They slowly made their way in the direction that would lead to Saffron's home. The enforcers had disappeared from sight on their mission to find Bishop or his remains.

"Dasha!" a familiar voice rang out from the woods.

Dasha froze at the sound of her sister's voice ringing through the air.

"Oh no," Saffron murmured.

Dasha tightened her grip on Saffron who turned to her. She gave a small smile and shook her head at her mate. It was time to tell her sister.

"It's okay. We are not going to hide what is between us any longer," Dasha said.

They continued on their path through the woods until Pola came bursting through the trees with Junior hot on her tail.

"Oh my goodness! Are you okay?" Pola exclaimed. Her wide eyes were frantic. She ran over to them, skidding to a halt in front of them. She paused, then looked between them and shook her head. "What's going on here? There's something you two have been holding back from me."

"You seriously need to ask?" Junior said, stopping next to Pola. He moved to Dasha's free side and took some of the weight off Saffron. He gave a healthy chuckle and tossed a wink at Dasha. "It's obvious that Saffron is Dasha's mate."

Dasha met her younger sister's gaze and prayed she wouldn't have a problem with it. Fate had determined they should be together. If she had an issue with it, she could take it up with fate.

"We were going to tell you," Saffron murmured. She took a step toward Pola then stopped. She glanced back at Dasha then turned back to Pola. "We were trying to figure out how to tell you without hurting you."

"Why would you think this would hurt me? My sister and my best friend." She looked away, lost in her thoughts. She glared at Dasha. "I don't see any claiming marks on her. You need to make an honest woman out of my bestie and treat her how she deserves to be."

Saffron squealed and rushed to Pola. She threw her arms around her, laughing and crying at the same time. Dasha relaxed. For a moment she thought Pola was going to be upset and be pissed at her.

"I'm so happy you are accepting of us," Saffron said, pulling back.

"I am. And the same goes for you. You better treat my sister right and love her forever." Pola laughed.

She moved over to Dasha where Saffron had vacated. She gave Dasha a hug and helped her along the trail. Dasha really didn't need her brother's and sister's help, but she'd take it anyway. This was a semi-joyous occasion.

"Don't worry. Dasha will get sick of me and my craziness soon." Saffron smiled at her over her shoulder. She led the way back to her home.

"Not in this lifetime," Dasha replied. She would never tire of her mate. For as long as they lived, she would love Saffron. Her bear gave a sharp snort of agreement.

"Now I want to know what happened." Junior leveled Dasha with his protective brother look. Even though he was the middle child, he took it upon himself to protect both his sisters. "Who was the bastard, and where is he so I can properly kick his ass?"

"Don't worry about it," Dasha said. She held back a grimace, trying to not show her pain. The fall had been brutal. It would be a miracle if Bishop survived. "The enforcers are looking for Bishop's body now."

"Bishop did this?" Pola gasped. "What was he doing here?"

"Apparently, he came to try to convince my mate that she should give him a chance instead of being with me." Dasha growled.

"And I've already told him twice that I didn't want to see him," Saffron interjected.

"When was the second time?" Pola asked.

"He had stopped by my shop earlier today. He said some really foul things, and I just told him I didn't want to see him. But he has it in his head that he's better for me then Dasha."

They broke out of the woods and walked across the yard. The lake was quiet, a few boats sailing off in the distance. A slight breeze blew past them, the scent of the water filling Dasha's senses. If she closed her eyes, she could pretend they had just been on a nice evening walk and not fighting for her mate with another bear. Seeing the look of love and adoration on Saffron's face sent a warm rush of emotions through her.

Without a thought, Dasha knew she would fight anyone for the love of her woman.

"Here we are," Junior announced.

They aimed for the steps that led up to Saffron's front porch.

"Will you two be all right by yourselves?" Pola asked.

"Of course. I'm not injured, and I can take care of Dasha's needs," Saffron replied. Her cheeks grew rosy red, her gaze flicking down to her feet.

"I'm not even going to go and make a joke since you're mating with my sister." Pola sighed. She released Dasha and turned to her. "Are you sure you don't need to shift again right now? That may help your healing."

"We're here if you want to. We can watch your back," Junior chimed in. He released Dasha and kept a steady eye on her as she took the few steps to the bottom stair.

Dasha faced her siblings while reaching out for her mate. She needed to have her hands on her. Her bear was still in her protective role. The fight with Bishop could have ended with either one of them submitting, or it could have ended in death

Saffron slid comfortably into her embrace.

There was no way in the seven hells Dasha would have submitted to Bishop and handed her mate over to him. She would rather face death than do that.

"Shifting may use up too much energy. I'll rest, though, and shift first thing in the morning. I should be good as new then." Dasha appreciated her siblings wanting to help, but she had one thing on her mind now that they were safely back at Saffron's home

"Are you—" Pola was shoved by Junior who wore a shit-eating grin.

"I'm sure our older sister knows what she wants, and it doesn't involve the two of us being around." He wagged his eyebrows.

The confusion on Pola's face quickly dissipated once she came to an understanding of what their brother was insinuating. She blew out a deep breath, pinching the bridge of her nose.

"This is going to take some getting used to," she muttered. "There are some things I just won't want to know."

"Understood." Saffron broke away and hugged Pola again. "I love you, bestie."

Dasha's heart swelled with the knowledge that her sister was happy for them. Pola glanced over Saffron's shoulder and winked at her. Dasha grinned at her little sister.

"I love you, too. Now make sure you take care of my sister. She can be very stubborn. Call me if see gives you any trouble."

"I promise to be the perfect patient." Dasha held up her hand.

Her siblings and Saffron laughed.

Dasha glanced at all of them. "What did I say that was so funny?"

"You following orders? We'll see about that!" Junior snorted.

"Get out of here, you two." Dasha playfully snarled at them.

It was well time for them to go. She wasn't going to expect the enforcers to come back with any news tonight. They would have to search the banks of the river to look for Bishop. The longer it took, the likelihood of them finding him would decrease.

Deep inside, Dasha had a feeling he'd survived. And if so, they would be seeing him again. He wasn't the type of bear who liked losing, and he sure as hell wouldn't want to be known as a grizzly who was defeated by a woman.

Men like him didn't take defeat lying down.

He would be back, and she would be ready for him.

"Come on, mate. Let's get you inside." Saffron came back to her side.

Dasha's bear gave a low growl. She liked the sound of Saffron calling them mate. Junior and Pola piled into his truck and drove off, leaving Dasha once again alone with her mate.

"Come, mate, we have unfinished business to attend to." Dasha tipped Saffron's chin up so their eyes could meet. They were intercepted before, and this time, nothing would keep her from claiming her.

"Oh, no. You need to rest and heal. No hanky-panky." Saffron pressed her palm to Dasha's sternum.

The warmth of her hand sank into Dasha's bare skin. Dasha closed the gap between them. She rested her hand on the small of Saffron's back to keep her close. The scent of her was growing thicker. Her mate was aroused, and no matter what words came out of her mouth, she wanted Dasha, too.

"What I need is to have my face buried between those sweet thighs of yours." Dasha bent down and pressed a soft kiss to Saffron's lips. Just the thought of lapping up Saffron's sweet nectar had her pulse racing. Saffron's body fell against hers. Dasha bit back a smile. She had her just where she wanted her. "Do you want my tongue deep in your pussy?"

"Yes," Saffron hissed.

Dasha brought her hands up and entwined her fingers into Saffron's thick hair. She held it firm, forcing Saffron's head to remain still. Even in the low light, she could make out Saffron's hooded eyes and parted lips. The scent of her arousal was overwhelming and triggered her inner beast. She had to have her now, and she had the intense need to claim this woman for all eternity.

"Do you want me to suck on your clit?" she asked.

"Yes."

"Claim you?"

"Yes." Saffron's answer ended in a hitch. She was panting and leaning her full weight on Dasha. With only her words, it would seem she was already close to her climax.

Dasha's body was flushed. Her thighs were coated with her desire, but her needs would have to wait. Her mate was top priority.

Always.

CHAPTER ELEVEN

Saffron exhaled sharply. The moment the door shut behind Dasha, her bear was on her. The clothing she had been wearing floated down to the floor in shards. Saffron welcomed the storm that was Dasha. Her mate's hands and lips were everywhere, and they weren't going to make it to the bedroom.

And Saffron was okay with that.

She loved when Dasha was in a frenzy. Saffron knew the sex with Dasha was going to be life-altering.

Saffron returned Dasha's kiss with the same heat. Dasha's tongue stroked hers while her hands cupped Saffron's plump bottom. Dasha bent down and lifted Saffron who automatically wrapped her legs around Dasha's waist. Their kiss grew deeper while Dasha walked them into the living room.

She tipped forward, and they crash-landed on Saffron's oversized couch. The weight of Dasha on top of her was intoxicating. She writhed underneath her, brushing her breasts against Dasha's. Their pebbled nipples teasing each other. Saffron cried out, needing more. Her body was flushed, excitement coursing through her.

Today she would become mated to the woman she loved.

When had she fallen in love with Dasha? She wasn't quite sure, but if she had to guess, she would say it was the first day she'd showed up at Dasha's house unannounced.

Dasha trailed hot kisses along Saffron's body. She made a pit stop at her breasts. She took her sweet time suckling them, teasing Saffron unmercifully. Dasha knew how to work her body until she was panting and begging for her release.

"Dasha," Saffron murmured.

She entwined her fingers into Dasha's thick, dark tresses. She parted her thighs as her mate kissed her stomach. Saffron knew exactly where she needed Dasha; her pussy ached with need. Her core dripped with the proof of her arousal. She was slick and ready to feel Dasha's tongue and fingers inside her.

She could have shouted for joy when Dasha arrived at her center. A pleased rumble vibrated from Dasha's chest. Her amber eyes glowed bright when she paused and looked up at Saffron. Her tongue snuck out and slid along her bottom lip. Saffron whimpered. Her hips thrust forward, demanding Dasha's attention.

"Look at all of this." Dasha's finger skated along Saffron's slit. She lifted it to show the white creamy substance coating it. Her tongue licked her finger clean. A groan escaped her, her eyes fluttering closed. "Open these pretty thighs of yours wider."

Saffron did as she was told. She cried out from the sensation of Dasha running her tongue along the same path her finger had taken. Saffron's fingers dove back into Dasha's hair. She held on tight while grinding her center against Dasha's face. She had already been desperate for her mate out on the porch from her dirty talk. She loved when Dasha was aggressive and took the lead. Which was most times they had sex. It was the bear in her, and Saffron loved it.

There was nothing sexier than being given instructions and then being rewarded with pleasure.

A gasp escaped her when Dasha sank two fingers inside her slick channel. Her mate slowly fucked her with them while she focused on suckling on her clit.

"God, yes," Saffron groaned.

She slid her hand to the back of Dasha's head where she could keep her in place. Her head was thrown back in the heat of passion, and she basked in the sensations coursing through her body.

She rode Dasha's tongue and fingers hard. Her breaths were coming in pants, her heart rate increasing. There was nothing else on Saffron's mind but reaching her release. She was teetering on the edge of ecstasy. A warm hand clamped down on one of Saffron's breasts. Dasha was making good use of her free hand and proving she was excellent at multitasking.

Saffron's hands flew above her, trying to find something to hold on to. She gripped the arm of the couch. She couldn't stay still with the erotic assault on her body. She turned her pleasure over to Dasha. A yelp escaped her the second Dasha pinched her nipple. She tugged and pulled on it, eliciting more cries to spill from Saffron's lips.

Tremors racked Saffron's body. Dasha's fingers were pumping inside her, hard and fast. Saffron dug her fingers into the couch, cries flowing from her mouth. Dasha took her to ledge of ecstasy. One tiny nip on her clit by Dasha's fangs, and it sent her careening into her orgasm. Her back arched off the couch, a long, drawn-out scream erupting from her.

She didn't know how long she lay there shaking and trembling from the aftereffects. Dasha released her clit but kept her fingers buried deep inside her. She raised her head and met Saffron's gaze.

Dasha lifted and crawled up her body. Her fingers managed to stay lodged where they were. She slid next to Saffron. Without a word, she claimed Saffron's lips. This kiss was deep and mind-blowing. Saffron tasted a hint of herself on Dasha's tongue.

Dasha slowly moved her fingers again.

She withdrew them until just the tip remained before pushing them deep. Saffron moaned. She reached up and cupped Dasha's face. She tore her lips from Dasha's. She inhaled deeply and stared unto her eyes.

"I love you," Saffron declared.

Dasha's fingers paused, completely submerged in Saffron's pussy.

"I love you, too," Dasha replied. She pressed a hard kiss to Saffron's lips. Her thumb stroked Saffron's clit. "You belong to me and I to you."

"I'm yours," Saffron breathed. She pressed her hips to Dasha's hand. "All of me. Take me."

She had waited to feel the sting of Dasha's bite, and now it was time. Her gaze dropped to the sight of Dasha's fangs peeking from under her lip. She turned her head away, presenting the column of her neck and shoulder. Dasha leaned her head down and nuzzled her face into the crook of her neck. Her warm tongue skated along Saffron's skin.

"You taste so sweet to me," Dasha's voice was muffled.

Her fingers continued their lazy strokes. Saffron was always amazed how Dasha could pull multiple orgasms from her. She should be embarrassed by the sounds coming from her core. With each thrust of Dasha's hand, her pussy was very verbal.

"I have to have you every day."

"You can have me whenever you want," Saffron gushed. Having Dasha make love to her daily was something she was all for.

"Good."

A sharp pain pierced her shoulder as Dasha bit down on her. Saffron at first cried out from the initial pain, but soon it dissipated, and nothing but pleasure filled her. This orgasm snuck up on her. Saffron threw her head back and cried out. Dasha's fingers pumped inside her, and she rode out the waves of her ecstasy. Her muscles clamped down on Dasha's fingers; they thrust into her.

Dasha lifted her head and released her shoulder. She lapped at the wound, where there was no pain. Saffron flopped back down on the couch, unable to catch her breath. She didn't even care what she looked like at the moment. The sheer magnitude of sensations coursing through her was overwhelming.

Dasha's fingers grew still. Saffron whimpered, loving the feeling of them inside her. She reached out and wrapped her fingers around Dasha's wrist, not wanting her to remove them. She opened her eyes and met Dasha's hooded gaze.

"My mate," Dasha breathed. She leaned down and took Saffron's lips in a gentle, sensual kiss. It was simple, but it relayed a strong message to Saffron.

Their bond was sealed, and they belonged together.

"My mate," Saffron echoed. Her entire body tingled, and there was no pain where Dasha had bitten her. She didn't know if this was part of the mating claim, but her body was flushed, and she felt like a new woman. One who had just had a spiritual and sexual awakening.

One who had a deep craving for her mate.

She needed more.

And she needed to taste her mate.

She let loose a whimper, her hips rising to make Dasha's fingers glide inside her. Saffron was almost frantic with her movements. She gripped Dasha's hand harder, needing another climax.

"What is this feeling I have?" Saffron asked softly. She couldn't explain what she felt at the moment. She'd never had this carnal need or lust harboring inside of her that felt so desperate. She had always been attracted to Dasha, but this was like lust to the hundredth power.

Dasha's amber eyes grew brighter. A grin spread her lips. She tried to withdraw her fingers, but Saffron's grip tightened, holding her in place. She chuckled, added a third, and pushed them fully inside Saffron.

"It would seem the mating fever is taking over you." Dasha withdrew her fingers, much to Saffron's displeasure. She positioned them with Saffron lying on top of her.

"Mating fever?" Saffron could barely concentrate. The velvety-smooth skin of Dasha's breasts pressed against hers was stealing her attention.

"The bite from your mate will trigger a visceral response where you will want to do nothing but mate."

"How long will this last?" Saffron whimpered. The intensity of her arousal was growing quiet painful. She rubbed her nipples against Dasha's, eliciting a moan from both of them. She didn't know how much of this she could bear.

"Every couple is different. We will have to bend to the will of fate until the fever burns out." Dasha's lips formed into a wide grin. "Come, my love. Give in to the fever and take what you need. We will get through this together."

CHAPTER TWELVE

"I will be in town and will stop by the shop," Dasha said.

"I can't wait to see you." Saffron sighed. She switched hands to hold her phone so she could peek out at the storefront. This afternoon, Capri and Moss were working, which allowed her to catch up on other things. As much as she loved serving the customers, she did have to put on her business owner hat and do things like payroll, ordering inventory, and paying bills.

"You just saw me this morning, how can you miss me already?"

Saffron went back into her small office and shut the door. The past two weeks had been amazing. She couldn't help the smile that filled her face. Her cheeks ached from the amount of smiling she had been doing since Dasha had claimed her.

Their mating fever had lasted five days. Saffron was still recovering from it. She ached in places she didn't even know existed. She'd lost count of the amount of orgasms Dasha had given her. For five long days she had remained in a constant state of intense arousal. Nothing was satisfying the urge to climax. Dasha had been claimed by the fever as well, but Saffron, as a human, had a more intense response.

When the fever had finally burned itself out of their systems, the two of them slept for almost forty-eight hours straight. Their families had been very supportive. Pola had explained the mating fever to Saffron's family who was extremely happy she had finally settled down. Both families rotated bringing them food so they would have something to eat. In between the bouts of lovemaking, they'd slept and ate.

Once they'd emerged from Saffron's home, she'd learned the entire bear community was made aware of the claiming. One of their first visitors was

Nick. The enforcer did not come with good news. They did not find Bishop's body. He hadn't been seen since. Saffron tried not to think of him. She just prayed that if he was still alive, he would leave her be.

"If you didn't know, I am mated to a very sexy bear and I want to spend all of my free time with her." Saffron sat at her desk and ignored the spreadsheets on the screen. Just thinking of their future together sent a warm rush of excitement through her. They were still trying to decide what to do with their homes. Dasha suggested the keep both. Each of them loved each other's home. When they wanted to be by the lake, they would stay at the lake house, and when they wanted to be secluded, they would go up in the mountains. It didn't take long to travel between them.

Dasha was planning a few works that would include the lake. Saffron couldn't wait for her to complete them. She was so talented, Saffron was sure they would sell immediately.

"You will see this bear when I come to town. I need to ship off a few paintings, then I'll be over."

Saffron glanced at the time and figured she could be done by then. Her crew could hold down the fort for a while.

"I'll see you then."

Once off the phone, Saffron had to force herself to concentrate. The payroll wasn't going to complete itself. She became lost in her work. She really did love owning her own business. It was a different pace from her old corporate job. Here she was the boss and could run things according to small-town time. The only deadline she had to be sure to make was payroll to ensure her employees were paid.

A knock at the door snagged her attention. About an hour had passed since she had hung up the phone with Dasha. Was she here already?

"Come in," Saffron called out.

Capri peeked her head through the door.

"Hey, Saffron, there's a guy to see you." Capri had been with Saffron since she had first opened the shop under her ownership.

"Oh, really? Did he say what he wanted?" Saffron frowned. It wasn't unusual to have solicitors stopping by to offer to sell her something for her business, but the timing was odd. Normally people stopped in first thing in the morning when she opened. Mid to late afternoon was practically unheard of. "Here I come."

Capri disappeared back though the doorway.

Saffron slid her sandals back on. At some point she had kicked them off while she was working.

Her gut twisted up in knots. She didn't know why she felt uneasy. She left her office and headed to the front of the store. There were no customers at the moment. Moss was in the midst of cleaning while Capri was restocking.

Saffron's gaze landed on the broad-shouldered figure by the door. The floor of her stomach gave way.

Bishop.

He casually locked the door and spun around.

"Hello, Saffron." A sadistic grin spread across his face. There was not a single scratch or scar on him. His amber eyes glowed bright, and his fangs were brandished. The growl that burst from him had Capri and Moss freezing in place. "You didn't think you could get rid of me that quickly, did you?"

Saffron glanced at her employees and uttered one word. "Run."

They both hesitated for a moment before taking off to the back of the store. There was an exit back there. She prayed they would call the police. Bishop gave a roar. His eyes flicked between her and her employees.

"I don't need them anyway." He stalked to the counter. "You're who I want."

"We thought you'd died." She tried to stall and get him to talk; maybe Capri and Moss would send some help her way. She was happy they were able to get away. She wouldn't know what she would do if Bishop hurt them. They were good people and didn't deserve to be caught up in this madness.

"You thought that bitch would be enough to take me out?" he hollered. He appeared to grow even larger as if he was about to shift.

She wouldn't stand a chance against a pissed-off, eight-foot-tall grizzly bear.

She tried to run, but he was too fast for her. He hopped over the counter and grabbed her by her hair. She cried out from the sharp pain in her head. Saffron swung her aims, determined to get away. A sinking feeling in the pit of her stomach told her she was a dead woman.

"Why can't you leave me alone?" she shouted.

He had the nerve to laugh at her feeble attempts to free herself. He wrapped one of his meaty arms around her waist and lifted her off her feet. Saffron kicked and screamed, hoping someone would hear her.

"I had you first." Spittle flew from his mouth.

She continued to struggle as he carried her toward the back where the large freezers were located. Fear unlike anything she'd ever known entered her. What was he going to do with her?

"Then that bitch came along and stole you."

"But we are mated now. Does that not mean anything?"

He paused for a brief moment, and Saffron had a small amount of hope that if he heard they were officially mated, it would change his mind and he would leave.

But that wasn't the case.

"If I can't have you, then that bitch will be without a mate!" Dark hair fluttered along his fore-arms, then receded.

Bishop was close to shifting, and Saffron wasn't in the mood to meet his bear up close and personal.

He opened the freezer and tossed her into it. She fell to her knees of the small, cold room. They kept the freezer below zero. Shelves with gallon drums of ice cream lined the walls around her.

She could already see the puffs of her breaths. Goosebumps lined her arms.

"You can't leave me in here, I'll freeze." She

scrambled to her feet. Her body was already growing chilly, and he hadn't even closed the door. Normally when she had to come in here, she would wear gloves and a fleece jacket that she kept hung on a hook outside the door.

"Don't worry. You'll get pretty warm soon." He slammed the door shut.

She let out a scream and banged on the steel door. There was no handle from the inside. There was a doorstop outside that they used to keep it open when they were storing the large tabs of ice cream. Never would she have thought she would need a freezer with a handle on the inside. Ice cream didn't magically get up and walk away.

She screamed repeatedly until her throat grew raw. Finally, she stood still and tried to see if she could hear him outside the door.

Nothing.

The door was solid steel.

You'll get pretty warm soon...

What the hell did that mean? Tremors racked her body. She ran her hands along her arms, trying to create warmth. The chill was already settling in. Was he talking about letting her freeze to death? She had heard stories that people who froze to death experienced a warming sensation before they died.

The only other way she would be warm would be—

Oh no.

He wouldn't, would he?

Bishop was deranged.

He was going to burn her building down with her locked up in it.

Saffron closed her eyes and hoped help came before it was too late.

If they didn't get her out soon, she was a goner. Visions of Dasha filled her mind. If this was the way she died, she was glad of one thing.

Following her gut to seek Dasha out was the best decision she'd ever made.

From that small instinct, she had got to mate with the most talented and beautiful woman she had ever known.

Looking around, she didn't see anything that could help her escape or keep her warm. She rubbed her arms harder and prayed for a miracle.

Fate couldn't have given her and Dasha this fabulous life only to take it away. She refused to believe that.

Saffron wrapped her arms around herself and thought of Dasha. Shivers racked her body uncontrollably. The heat that always spread through her when she thought of her bear should be plenty enough to ward off the cold air.

CHAPTER THIRTEEN

"We'll make sure it's wrapped up really good. This is an amazing painting, Dasha." Jack stared at her work.

She had sold a painting that she was a little behind in sending off. She always brought her work to Jack who specialized in specialty shipping.

Dasha never knew how to respond when someone admired her work. It was her living and her passion, but she wasn't one who liked to receive praise. She just did what she loved, and there were people willing to pay for it.

"Um, thank you?"

"You have real talent, girl. I see why people are beating down at your door to get their hands on your work." He grinned and placed the painting on the floor behind him. He turned back and rang up her transaction. It was a little pricey to ship through him, but she trusted that her work would arrive to her client unscathed. For the amount of money she was paid for her work, Jack was worth it.

Dasha offered a small smile while she signed the receipt. He handed her back her credit card which she slid back into her wristlet.

"I'll be back in a few days. I have a three-piece series I need to mail out," she said.

"Oh, that sounds interesting. One day I may have to save up some money to purchase one of your paintings. You're going to be famous one day, and I would love to already have a something of yours." He laughed.

"Well, I do know the artist and I can get you a really great deal."

He barked a hard laugh and slapped a hand on the counter. "I'll take you up on it one day."

"Thanks again, Jack. I'll see you later," Dasha said. She gave him a wave and headed out of his store. She inhaled sharply and picked up on the faint scent of smoke.

Shaking her head, she walked back to her SUV that was parked on the street in front of Jack's store. He was located two streets over from Saffron's ice cream shop. Now that she had concluded her business, she could go pick up her beautiful mate and take her out to lunch.

She jogged around the front of her truck and paused. She glanced over at the sidewalk and took in two men and a woman frantically running down toward the corner of the street. They rounded the corner and were no longer in sight.

That was weird.

The sound of a fire engine blaring its horn. That explained the scent of smoke she'd picked up. Something must be on fire.

The hairs on the back of her neck stood up to attention.

Dasha opened the driver's door of her vehicle and tossed her wristlet onto the passenger seat. She paused and kept a hand on the door as a feeling pulsed inside her.

Fear.

She frowned, not sure where this was coming from. She wasn't scared of anything at the moment.

Her bear paced. Her beast was unsettled and rumbled deep in her chest.

"What is going on?" Dasha murmured.

Saffron, her beast whispered.

Dasha froze in place. Was that fear she experienced not her own? Was that Saffron's feelings? There were some accounts of mates sharing a special bond where they were able to pick up on each other's emotions.

She reached in the back pocket of her jeans and pulled out her cell. She slid her finger across the glass screen and opened it. She hit Saffron's number and put her phone up to her ear.

"Come on, babe. Answer." She listened to it ring before it went over to the generic voicemail.

That didn't sit well with her.

She hit Saffron's number.

Again, no answer. Saffron's voicemail picked up.

Dasha swung into her truck and tossed her phone down next to her wristlet. She would just go to the shop. She was sure they were probably busy and Saffron hadn't heard her cell ring. That was possible.

But the nausea that took hold of her said otherwise.

She drove the way to Saffron's shop, and the fear was becoming overwhelming. She tightened her hand on the steering wheel. The scent of the smoke was growing thicker. She turned the final corner where Lick or Bite was located.

Her heart slammed against her chest at the sight of the fire engines and police cars parked in front of Saffron's shop. The building was engulfed in flames.

Dasha hit the brake, unable to go any farther along the road due to the police blocking it off. She pulled off to the side of the road and parked her SUV. She killed the engine and exited. She slammed the door and took off running toward the building. There was a crowd of onlookers standing across the street.

Dasha frantically scanned the crowd, trying to find any sight of Saffron. Her gaze landed on two people.

Saffron's employees, Capri and Moss, were standing next to a police car and were speaking with two cops. Dasha ran in their direction.

"Excuse me," she muttered, pushing through the people standing watching the flames coming from the building. Within a few minutes, she had made her way to them. "Capri. Moss. Where is Saffron?"

They turned to her, and the bottom of her stomach dropped. Capri's eyes were red-rimmed, and tears streaked her cheeks.

"I don't know. I think she's still in there. There was this man—"

"Excuse me. Who are you?" the cop asked.

"I'm Saffron Dakota's mate," she growled. Her bear surged against her chest, trying to break free. She pushed her beast back down. She, the human, needed to remain in control for the moment.

"Okay. I'm Sergeant Sidney." He swallowed hard. His eyes widened as if he realized she was a shifter and trying to remain calm. "From the report these two just gave me, a large male fitting the description of the missing Bishop Milligan, was in the Lick or Bite. Ms. Dakota was able to get them out."

"Has anyone made it in there?" Dasha's gaze turned toward the building. The flames and smoke reached for the sky. Her bear roared, demanding they go after their mate. "Has anyone captured Bishop?"

"We've been in contact with the clan's enforcers. They have been brought up to speed on the situation." He faced the building and motioned to the firefighters. "They haven't been able to go in there yet. The flames are too much. They need to get them under control first."

"She's in there," Dasha murmured. She felt it

deep into her soul that her mate was somewhere locked in that building. She couldn't stand by and wait to go in there and find her dead.

Her bear roared, demanding they shift. They would go in there and save her.

Dasha took off toward the ice cream shop. She ignored Sidney's shout for her to come back. There was no way she would sit idle waiting for the humans to rescue her human.

Another growl rippled from her. She sped up and raced past the yellow safety tape the law enforcement had positioned, creating a perimeter around the building. She ignored everyone yelling at her.

She gave in to her shift.

Her bear took over from her, and her shift was completed within seconds. This was an emergency. Dasha threw back her head, letting out a massive roar. Her clothes lay in tattered remains on the ground around her. She kicked them away and glanced up at the building. The people around her scattered, spreading out, far from her. She couldn't care less what they thought.

She needed to rescue her mate.

Dasha rushed to the front door and rose on her hind legs and pounded on it with her front legs. The door gave way under her force. Thick dark smoke poured out of the door and drifted to the sky.

She fell back down on all fours and made her way inside the building. Flames ate up the walls, while the ceiling was full of smoke. Her lungs burned slightly, but Dasha ignored it. She had to find Saffron. There was no sign of her in the front of the store.

Dasha's eyes watered from the smoke. She blinked and kept moving. It was dark aside from the flames. She moved to Saffron's office where the door was open. She went inside and didn't see any signs of her. She grew frustrated, but then again was grateful she hadn't found Saffron's body anywhere.

She turned to leave but had to jump back. The ceiling gave way, parts of it falling to the floor. The sounds of the flames overcoming the building were deafening. Dasha continued her search for her. In her gut, she knew Saffron was still here.

Dasha continued on. She didn't know how much longer she would make it. The smoke was getting thick. She coughed and had to pause. The air was growing thin in there, but she refused to leave without her mate with her. She bent down as far as she could and crawled through the rest of the shop. The small little kitchen was empty, and the little break room revealed nothing. The only other place she could think to check would be the freezer.

Dasha stood still and tried to focus on breathing. She wheezed, inhaling smoke. Her lungs were burning significantly, but she was determined to search every inch of this place until she was either sure there were no signs of Saffron or she found her.

Dasha's paws grew heavier to lift as she made her way to the freezer. The thick steel door was locked from the outside. She pawed at it and was unable to get it unlock with her claws. They did nothing but scape along the door, missing the lock mechanism.

She snarled, frustrated that her large paws couldn't open the door. There was no way she could tear her way through this door. She was growing weaker from the heat, the smoke, and thinning air.

She was going to have to shift back to her human form.

Give me control, she begged her beast. Her animal was stubborn and snarled. *I don't want to hear it. You can't open the door. I can. We have to check this out. Saffron could be in there. She needs us.*

Her bear hesitated but soon relented. Saffron was more important.

Her body contorted while the thick fur disappeared within the pores of her skin. In seconds, she was once again in her human form.

"Shit," she exhaled. She thought it had been hard to breathe when she was in her bear form, but it was even worse in her human form. Dasha was going to have to work quickly. The building wasn't going to last long. A crash sounded near the front of the store. A section of the ceiling crashed down. She turned back to the door, remaining on her knees where the fresh air was and unlocked it.

Dasha pulled it open, a coughing fit overtaking her. She peered into the freezer, and her heart thumped louder.

. There was lone figure lying on the floor.

"Saffron!" she shouted. She stood and propped the door open. She had to be fast. She couldn't take the risk that the door would slam shut. Then they both would be trapped inside.

Dasha made her way into the freezer. The air was chilly. She knelt by Saffron and rested a hand on her shoulder. She pulled her onto her back and breathed a sigh of relief at the sight of her thready pulse at the base of her neck.

"Come on, love. Let's get out of here," Dasha murmured. She wasn't going to worry why her mate was unconscious. At least she had a pulse. She would get them out of here, then they would figure this out.

Dasha lifted her mate from the floor and kept her close to her. Saffron's skin felt like ice. Dasha braved the smoke and walked through the doorway of the freezer and made her way to the back door. The door was unlocked, and she was able to get it open. She exited through it and immediately inhaled deeply. She coughed as she strode away from the building. There was a small wooded area that separated this street that held businesses and a residential area.

Dasha made it to the grass, collapsing onto her knees. Coughing racked her as she tried to inhale. Tears flowed down her cheeks, blurring her vision. The smoke had stung her eyes, and she wasn't sure how she'd managed to get out of there.

"We need help!" she shouted. She screamed again, needing someone to come to them. She fell to her side, lying next to Saffron. She reached for her mate and rubbed her face. She had nothing to place over her to try to keep her warm until help could come for them. She tried to use her body heat to warm Saffron. "Help!"

She turned back to Saffron and used her hands to rub her arms. Her skin was a dusky color, and her lips were dark blue. Dasha didn't like any of this. She pressed a kiss to her mate's lips.

"Come on, baby. Wake up," she begged. She blinked hard, tears falling down her face.

"Dasha!" a gruff voice called out her name.

She glanced up toward the trees, and her mouth dropped open in disbelief. Nick, Sega, and Abe broke through the woods, practically dragging a shackled Bishop.

"Is she all right?" Nick asked. He beelined it to her.

She didn't take her eyes from Bishop. He shot her a nasty glare, and she returned it with one of her own. A growl rumbled from her. She sat up, but Nick held his hand up and stood in her view of Bishop.

"Stand down, Dasha. Your mate needs you."

Those words brought her attention back to Saffron.

"I've been calling for help." Her voice cracked as she tried to speak.

Nick knelt by her and pressed two fingers to the

side of her neck. His gaze roamed Saffron for a moment before he stood. "Stay with her. I'll send the medics back here."

"Thank you." She brushed Saffron's dark strands away from her face.

"Don't worry about Milligan. He's going to pay for what he's done." Nick rested a hand on her shoulder then jogged off toward the front of the building.

She glanced back down at Saffron and pressed a kiss to her forehead. Saffron's body trembled in her arms. She was so cold and needed to be warmed up. She glanced back down and caught her mate's open eyes locked on her.

"You came for me," Saffron whispered. Her teeth were chattering. She leaned into Dasha, her body shaking hard.

"Of course I did," Dasha murmured. She tightened her hold on her. There was nothing that would keep her from Saffron.

"I love you," Saffron said. Tears filled her eyes and spilled onto her cheeks. She coughed, and audible wheezing could be heard.

Dasha pressed a finger to her lover's lips.

"Don't talk," she said. Her voice was strained, and a sharp pain rippled down her throat. She rested her forehead on Saffron's. Relief filled her that her mate was alive. This could have ended completely differently. "And just so you know, Bishop is in enforcer custody."

Saffron's body jerked even harder as she sobbed. Dasha held her until she had to let her go so the EMTs could come check her out. The medics lifted her on their cart, secured. Even though Saffron protested going to the hospital, Dasha insisted she go. She wasn't going to rest comfortably until she was told Saffron was still healthy.

Saffron's hand shot out for her. Dasha took it and entwined their fingers together. She pressed a kiss to the back of her cold hand.

"Don't leave me," Saffron whispered.

The medics had wrapped her up in blankets, and her face was the only thing visible. Dasha didn't know how her hand slipped out from underneath the blankets. They had brought her one, too, and she wrapped it around her body, toga style.

"I'll never leave you, babe. You have me for eternity."

EPILOGUE

Saffron sat next to Dasha with their hands entwined. She had never been a witness to a shifter's sentencing before, but today, she wouldn't miss this one for the world. It had been a month since the day her business had burned down.

Apparently, after setting the fire, Bishop had settled in the yard of a couple who were out of town so he could watch his handiwork from afar. The enforcers had arrived at the scene and quickly picked up his trail.

They were currently located in one of the buildings on the clan property where the alpha would address the clan and render Bishop's punishment. The room was buzzing with low conversations. She and Dasha sat in the front row. Together, they would face Bishop when he was brought before the clan and the alpha.

Butterflies fluttered inside Saffron's stomach. She wasn't sure why, but she just knew she wanted this day over with. It had seemed to take forever for this day to come, and now that it was here, she wanted it over so she and Dasha could go on with their lives. Unlike the human justice system, they didn't take long to render punishments and sentencing. The alpha was the law.

"You okay?" Dasha murmured. She squeezed Saffron's hand tight.

Saffron jerked her head in a nod.

"Yeah, I'm good." She looked over her shoulder and peeked in on her family sitting a few rows behind them. Her parents and brother sat together. Her brother, Jaco, winked at her. She smiled at him and tossed one his way. Dasha's family sat on the other side of her.

Saffron carefully glanced to the other side of the room and saw Bishop's family sitting in the front row on their side. From what Saffron had heard, they had tried to get the alpha to let Bishop off with a warning.

It would appear the alpha wasn't one to take bribes.

The door off to the side opened, and a woman, tall and muscular, walked out. Her hair was long and dark. This was a woman who demanded respect. Saffron had heard of Eddie but had never had the opportunity to meet her before. Another woman, the clan's beta, Selan Rawlyn, followed Eddie. They both took a seat at a small half-circle table. In front of the table was a single chair that faced them.

The conversations died off as everyone waited for the alpha to speak.

"Bring in the prisoner," the alpha's voice shot out. It was husky and deep. The woman scanned the room and nodded to everyone whose gaze she met.

An enforcer from the back walked over to the entrance at the rear. He stepped outside, and they had to wait. The tension in the air grew thicker. Saffron inhaled then blew out a deep breath. A moment later, the door reopened, and Bishop was shackled around his ankles, his wrists, and a had device locked around his neck.

He walked in, and his gaze landed on her. His lip twisted up in the corner.

"Do not look at her. Look at me," Eddie snapped.

Goosebumps appeared on Saffron's arms at the power of the woman's voice. He pulled his gaze from Saffron and turned to the alpha, doing as he was commanded. Sega and Abe led him down to the chair.

"Take a seat."

"I'd rather stand," Bishop replied.

"Very well. This won't take long." Eddie adjusted herself in her chair and crossed her legs. She eyed the bear shifter before continuing. "Bishop Milligan. You have been charged with attempted murder of a human, arson, and breaking the shifter mating code. You deliberately pursued a woman who was claimed by another bear, and that is against our laws."

Bishop didn't say a word. He stood with his legs as far as they would go due to his shackles.

Saffron's heart raced. She couldn't look away from the scene before her. Apparently, the human laws allowed shifters to take care of their own when it came to crimes. Bishop wouldn't have to face the human authorities. Eddie, his alpha, would be the judge and the jury.

"I've looked at all of the testimonies and the evidence of the crimes committed. Bishop Milligan, you have been found guilty of the crimes I've already mentioned. You will serve thirty years in Purgatory Prison to pay for your crimes."

Gasps went out around.

Saffron sat in shock.

He was going to prison.

She and Dasha would be able to live their lives in peace.

"That is ridiculous," a man shouted. He was the exact image of Bishop. He had more wrinkles on his face and a few gray strands of hair. This must be Bishop's father.

"Stand down, Milligan," Selan barked. She eyed the older man and held up a hand. "Unless you want to do some time along with your son."

He sputtered but then sat.

"Do you have anything to say for yourself?" Eddie asked.

Bishop turned his head and again met Saffron's gaze, but this time, Saffron wasn't afraid of him.

"I said don't look at her."

He turned back to the alpha.

"No, ma'am. I don't have anything to say."

"If you have nothing to say, then your sentencing has been concluded. Remove him and prepare him for Purgatory." The alpha stood from her chair as Bishop was led back out.

The room exploded with chatter. Bishop's family shot her a dirty look before stalking out. She shook her head, unable to believe they would be upset with her. It was their son who'd created this mess.

Saffron turned to Dasha in shock.

"That's it?" she asked.

"What more did you want?" Dasha stood and pulled Saffron up. She wrapped an arm around her waist and brought her close to her. She cupped Saffron's face in her hands. She pressed a kiss to Saffron's lips, a small smile on hers. "Our laws and punishments are straight to the point."

Their families surrounded them, smiling and congratulating them that their attacker had been put away. Saffron leaned into Dasha, a smile on her lips. She barely heard the conversation that was being held.

All she could think about was this nightmare was over. She and Dasha had to be treated for smoke inhalation, and Saffron had to deal with hypothermia. Lucky enough, she didn't have any frostbite since the power had been cut to the building once the firefighters arrived at her shop.

The Lick or Bite was totaled. But would return soon. She had received the insurance money and was going to fix her baby up and make it even better than before. She had some ideas on how she could improve her ice cream shop.

She and Dasha had finally came up with a routine on where they would be living. Their primary home would be the house on the lake. They both loved the area and used Dasha's cabin as their getaway spot, and she would go up there to work.

Life was good.

"How about it?" Dasha asked.

Saffron blinked and turned her attention to Dasha.

"How about what?" she asked. She blushed, sensing their family staring at her. She must have missed something.

"My mother suggested we all go to her house for dinner to celebrate." Pola nudged her. "What are you daydreaming about?"

Saffron smiled, and Pola rolled her eyes.

"Don't worry, it was all PG," Saffron teased. She turned back to Dasha and nodded. "I think it would be a great idea to go back to your parents' for dinner."

With the plan solidified, they made their way out of the building. They all agreed to meet at the Primes' home. Dasha and Saffron waved and walked to Dasha's SUV. Dasha escorted her to the side and paused.

Saffron felt an unlimited amount of love for this woman before her. She wrapped her arms around Dasha's waist and smiled.

"Have I told you how much I love you today?" she asked playfully. She leaned up and offered her lips for a kiss.

Dasha didn't disappoint her and covered her lips with hers. The kiss was deep and sensual. It completely took Saffron's breath away. Dasha pulled back and rested her forehead on Saffron's.

"It's been a few hours, but I'm always up to hear it often," Dasha replied.

"I love you. I love you. I love you."

Love Saffron and Dasha's story? Well, continue on to Pola's story in Claimed by Her Bear! It's available to read NOW!

ABOUT THE AUTHOR

Ariel Marie is an author who loves the paranormal, action and hot steamy romance. She combines all three in each and every one of her stories. For as long as she can remember, she has loved vampires, shifters and every creature you can think of. This even rolls over into her favorite movies. She loves a good action packed thriller! Throw a touch of the supernatural world in it and she's hooked!

Sign up for Ariel Marie's newsletter!
Scan the QR Code to get all the latest news from Ariel Marie!

For more information visit:

www.thearielmarie.com

The Nightstar Shifters

No wolf can resist the call to mate.

Strong female wolves are in search of their mate. The desire is strong for these women who long to find the one person meant for them.

They are fierce and determined, putting their trust in fate.

If you love lesbian wolf shifter romance filled with action and adventure, then you will love the Nightstar Shifters series.

Ready to start the Nightstar Shifters? Click HERE to download book one!

<u>The Immortal Reign Series</u>

Vampires and Humans. Are they meant to be together? One drop of blood will control their futures.

After the war between vampires and humankind, Earth was never the same. This new world was dangerous, and vampires were on the hunt for their fated mates. The installation of the draft should have made things simpler, but all it did was create chaos.

Humans didn't want to conform to the new ways of life.

Vampires had no problems making them.

Enter this new dark and sexy world full of lesbian vampire romance. The Immortal Reign series is an adult-themed paranormal romance that you will want to sink your teeth into. If you love action-packed, sizzling hot wlw romances, then this is the series for you.

Start the Immortal Reign series today! Click HERE to download book one!

ALSO BY ARIEL MARIE

<u>The Montana Grizzlies</u>

Hot For Her Bear

Claimed by Her Bear

Bound to Her Bear

Marked by Her Bear

<u>The Nightstar Shifters</u>

Sailing With Her Wolf

Protecting Her Wolf

Sealed With A Bite

Hers to Claim

Wanted by the Wolf

Taming Her Mate

<u>The Immortal Reign series</u>

Deadly Kiss

Iced Heart

Royal Bite

Wicked Allure

<u>Blackclaw Alphas (Reverse Harem Series)</u>

Fate of Four

Bearing Her Fate (TBD)

<u>The Midnight Coven Brand</u>

Forever Desired

Wicked Shadows

<u>Paranormal Erotic Box Sets</u>

Vampire Destiny (An Erotic Vampire Box Set)

Moon Valley Shifters Box Set (F/F Shifters)

The Dragon Curse Series (Ménage MFF Erotic Series)

<u>The Dark Shadows Series</u>

Princess

Toma

Phaelyn

Teague

Adrian

Nicu

<u>Stand Alone Books</u>

Dani's Return

A Faery's Kiss

Tiger Haven

Searching For His Mate

A Tiger's Gift

Stone Heart (The Gargoyle Protectors)

Saving Penny

A Beary Christmas

Howl for Me

Birthright

Return to Darkness

Red and the Alpha

The Iron Oath